MW00769911

COLLATERAL

Debt Collection, Book One

Roxie Rivera

Night Works Books
College Station, Texas

Night Works Books
College Station, Texas 77845
www.roxierivera.com

Collateral (Debt Collection #1) / Roxie Rivera.1st ed.
ISBN 978-1-63042-023-9

For Joey and Marcos, the two most loyal, overprotective and wildly funny brothers a girl could ask for...

1 Chapter one

"Aston, do you want me to come inside with you?"

Filled with dread, I glanced away from the rusted façade of Merkurie Motors & Towing to the driver's seat where Marley eyed me with concern. "Is it pathetic that I want to say yes and ask you to hold my hand?"

My best friend bit her lower lip and studied the garage where an illegal chop shop allegedly operated. "It's not the kind of place I would want to visit after dark. Actually, it's exactly the kind of place Dad has forbidden me to visit, like, ever."

That tidbit didn't fill me with the warm and fuzzies. Spider, Marley's stepdad, was the vice president of the Calaveras, Houston's scariest outlaw motorcycle gang. When he gave an instruction like that, it was for a good reason.

The *snick* of a seat belt unbuckling drew my attention. Marley slipped her arm out of the belt and tugged the hair elastic from her wrist. As she gathered her auburn hair into a high ponytail, she said, "I'm coming with you."

"But Spider-"

"His name will keep us safe," she replied with a look. "This crew knows better than to mess with Octavio Ruiz's kid." She glanced away from me and tugged her keys from the ignition. "Their boss wouldn't like it either. Not after what he did for me."

A few weeks earlier, Marley had been kidnapped with a coworker and his son who owed a debt to a drug cartel. In the standoff that followed, she had nearly been shot by a cartel assassin gone rogue. Besian Beciraj, the notorious Albanian mob boss and loan shark reputed to own this auto shop, had thrown himself into the line of fire to save her. He had taken a bullet meant for Marley and had barely survived the shooting.

She hadn't been very forthcoming about why this man she hardly even knew would so something so heroic, and I hadn't pressed the issue. We had been friends so long I could read her easily. She didn't know what to think about the mob boss and she didn't want to talk about it. When she was ready, she would say something. Until then? I was staying out of her business.

"Look, we probably won't even get inside the shop tonight. Ben Beciraj, the guy who runs this place, isn't going to be very enthusiastic about two girls like us wandering into the middle of this outrageously illegal operation."

"I have to try." Gripping the door handle, I tried to work up the nerve to get out of her car. "Baby has been missing since eight. It's nearly midnight. If I don't get in there now, I might lose her forever because that asshole stepbrother of mine wanted to get back at me by taking her and deliberately leaving the keys in the ignition in that awful part of town."

Marley's eyebrows arched. "You realize you sound like you're talking about a person, right? It's a car, Aston."

"It was my father's car. His *favorite* car," I added, thinking of all the Sunday mornings I had spent at his side, buffing and polishing the '63 Aston Martin DB5. Of all the cars in his vast collection, Baby had been the one he had loved best. "He named me after that car. I learned to drive in Baby. I had my first kiss in that car." Swallowing hard, I choked back the tears that threatened to overtake me. "I sat in the driver's seat of that car when Daddy told me he was dying." Gritting my teeth, I shook my head. "I'm not losing her now."

Marley sighed loudly and reached over to squeeze my hand. "Even if they let us inside, and even if you're able to negotiate for the car, it won't be cheap."

With a careless shrug, I opened the door. "I guess it's a good thing I'm so disgustingly rich."

She snorted indelicately. "Embrace that bitchy attitude you worked so hard to lose in high school, Aston. You're going to need it in there. We're walking straight into the lion's den."

"Don't you mean eagle's nest?" I asked, thinking of the double-headed eagle symbol the Albanian crime family had chosen as their own. Though I wasn't part of this seedy underbelly, I wasn't naive or uninformed. I understood that a parallel world existed to the privileged one I lived in and enjoyed. My stepbrother Calvin had been flirting with the dark side of the city for years. Now I was the one getting burned by his fascination with these criminals.

Side by side, we crossed the quiet street and made our way to the garage. We exchanged nervous glances as the whine of saws and the snapping zips of impact tools filled the night. Gulping down my fear, I balled up my fist and beat on the closest garage door. When that received no answer, I kicked the door while pounding on it, suddenly glad I had chosen the red suede pumps with metal toe points that morning.

The noise inside the shop grinded to a halt. Seconds later, I winced when the heavy metal door started to rise and made a terrible screeching noise. Inch by inch, the rising door revealed a man. First a pair of big, dirty work boots and then a pair of jeans flecked with oil and dark stains on the knees. A white muscle shirt smudged with grease and grime came into view next.

But it was the brawny arms emblazoned with tattoos from knuckles to shoulders that enthralled me. I had interacted with Marley's stepdad enough to be accustomed to the sight of gang ink, but the sleeves on this man were breathtaking. I noticed the marks on his neck and the tattoo on the underside of his wrist. I tried not to think about what types of things a man might have to do to earn that double-headed eagle and an invitation to the inner circle of the mob boss who had saved Marley's life.

Up and up, my gaze drifted along the imposing height of him and settled on his handsome face. A wicked thrill fluttered through my belly. He had a hard face, his jaw angled and his nose sporting the telltale signs of having been broken at least once. His dark, unkempt hair fell carelessly around his ears. He had eyes like jade, the color pale, but they seared me with their intensity. When he crossed his powerful arms, the muscles flexing menacingly, I couldn't help but wonder what it would feel like to have them wrapped around me.

"Ben Beciraj?" I hazarded an educated guess.

"Yeah. What the hell do you want?" His gruff, irritated voice set off a strange quivering sensation in my chest. I couldn't tell if it was because I was terrified or excited. To be honest, it was probably a bit of both. The dangerous aura surrounding this man warned me to be careful, but I kept looking at those big, scarred hands of his and thinking about them touching me in the most intimate ways. "Well?"

Startled by his rough voice, I shot a petrified look Marley's direction before working up the courage to meet the man's glare. "My name is-"

"I know who you are."

I blinked at the rude way he had cut me off. "How?"

"I recognized your face from all those society page stories."

"You read the society section?"

He issued a clipped laugh. "What's wrong? You shocked that someone like me can actually read?"

Frowning at his bitter remark, I decided not to go there. Instead, I stated my case. "Look, my car was stolen earlier this evening. My stepbrother left it in a parking lot outside one of those gross strip clubs he likes to visit. When he came out, it was gone."

"And?" His stony gaze turned cold. "How the fuck is any of that my problem?"

His mean reply squashed whatever fascination I had with him. "Are you really going to stand there and act like you don't know why I'm beating on your garage door at midnight? Like I don't know you and your little crew of thieving miscreants stole my car and have it locked away somewhere in this ratty shop of yours?" Lifting my chin and throwing back my shoulders, I remembered Marley's advice. "Give me my car-or else you're going to regret it."

The corner of his mouth twitched. Was it amusement? Did he find my threat funny? Or was it something else, something far more sinister? Was that tiny, almost imperceptible twitch the only warning I would be given?

"I doubt that very much."

"Yeah?" Playing the only card I had, I raised the cell phone gripped tightly in my hand. "How many cops do you think dispatch will send out here when I tell them my name?" I started to dial 9-1-1. "Five? Ten? Maybe I'll just call the mayor directly-"

He took a menacing step forward. "Hang up. *Now."*

"Or what?" I refused to be cowed by this tattooed brute. "You'll hit me?"

His head snapped back as if I had slapped him. His throat bobbed, and he clenched his fists at his sides. "I've never hit a woman in my life. Instead of threatening me with the police, you should learn to pay your fucking debts. This car has been on the repo list for two weeks. You had your chance to make things right."

"Wait. What?" I lowered my hand, the phone call forgotten. "What debts? I don't owe a penny to anyone!"

Mr. Ink and Muscles narrowed his eyes. After an uncomfortable moment of scrutiny, he stepped back into the garage and crooked a finger in my direction. "Let's talk about this some place more private."

I took a step forward, but Marley clasped my wrist. She shook her head. "No."

Ben's jaw tightened. "You're both safe here. I give my word." **In** case we doubted what his word was worth, he eyed Marley. "My boss would have my balls in a jar on his desk if anything happened to that one." Then, as an afterthought, he added, "Spider and his M.C. would burn this garage to the ground with me inside it if Besian didn't catch me first."

Marley and I shared a look. She had told me that this tightly knit crew of men adhered to a code of honor that went back centuries. Even though this guy could easily snap my neck with those strong hands, he wasn't going to hurt me. I believed that much.

We entered the garage together, but he motioned for Marley to wait near a toolbox. He called out to the group of men watching us with interest in a language I had never heard. I assumed it was Albanian but wished it had been Mandarin, French or Russian, languages I spoke fluently and easily.

A giant man who had been hiding at the rear of the group elbowed his way through the small crowd. I tilted my head back to take in all of him. He was taller than all of his companions by a foot and had shoulders nearly as wide as the SUV behind him, but it wasn't his uncommon height that held my attention. No, it was the gnarly scars arcing across the right side of his face. I didn't know what type of weapon would make such jagged wounds, but I had a feeling this man had suffered a brutal and vicious attack, one that had cut him from scalp to shoulder, judging by the thick scar running down to the collar of his shirt.

"Devil is going to watch your friend. You?" Ben pointed at me. "You're coming with me."

Marley squeezed my hand before we separated. She didn't seem the least bit intimidated by the hulking beast who had been assigned babysitting duties. Considering what I knew of her stepfather's friends, I wasn't that surprised. At times like this, I envied her rather harsh upbringing. She understood so much more of the world than I ever would and navigated the bumpy waters of life much better than me.

My belly wobbled as I followed Ben into the office on the far left side of the garage. The moment I stepped inside the room, he slammed the door shut behind me and pinned me against it. He used his larger frame to box me in and flattened his palms against the cold metal at my back. I sucked in a shuddery, nervous breath and stared up at him.

We were so close his body heat seeped into me. His hard chest grazed my breasts and the scent of him, a masculine blend of sweat, denim, and leather that smelled of hard work, ignited something primal and feminine inside me. None of the men I encountered in my day-to-day life had ever looked at me the way he did. None of them would have dared to behave in such a dominant, alpha way either.

His pale eyes glinted with frustration-and lust. I wasn't sure what was going to happen now. He was going to kiss me or hurt me. Or maybe both.

Ben Beciraj didn't know what to do with the infuriatingly beautiful woman he had pinned to the door. He was torn between wanting to snarl at her and wanting to kiss her. He squashed the latter impulse. This wasn't the kind of girl who would welcome his attention. She was pretty and rich and existed in a league so far outside his own they weren't even in the same universe. She probably wanted to recoil at having someone so grubby and obviously beneath her breathing the same air.

When all that racket had started outside the garage, the very last thing he had expected to find was Aston Fucking McNeil, Houston's favorite socialite, beating on his damned door. He had been sure it was one of the boosters coming by with an extra car. Though the team of thieves had gone out tonight with a list of specific targets, it wasn't unusual for the boys to come across an easy mark. Motivated by money, they would swipe any car possible for extra cash.

But what motivated this girl? He didn't know, and it unsettled him. He had learned to read people at a very early age but he couldn't get a fix on Aston. That surprised him. His ability to figure out a person with a single look came in useful for a young boy running the halls of a notorious brothel. Some of the men who frequented that place had a taste for something other than the high class whores who offered their services. Dropping a man with one well-placed punch had been another skill he had learned at an early age.

Thinking of the cruel, stark upbringing he had known, he studied the young woman pressed between the door and his body. She didn't belong here. This wasn't her world. Hell, it wasn't even Marley's world. She might be the stepdaughter of one of the meanest sons of bitches in the city, but she had been greatly shielded from the horrors of Spider's life.

Until that night she had been kidnapped, Besian had been shot, and he had been tasked with cleaning up the crime scene at the pawn shop to protect the family. As long as he had known the boss, Besian had never, not once, shown interest in someone like Marley. He'd always preferred the wild, adventurous women who danced at his clubs. He liked things simple and easy-a few quick fucks, some cash and gifts to signal the end and a clean getaway.

But that young woman standing in the garage under Devil's guard? Ben couldn't wrap his head around that one. And this young woman? The one peering up at him with mistrust and curiosity? He really couldn't wrap his head around her.

The scent of something floral and flirty tickled his nose. It smelled expensive, the notes bright and clean and unmarred by the stringent bite of alcohol used in the cheaper drugstore perfumes he was used to smelling on the dancers at the clubs their family owned. He fought the urge to bend low and inhale her sweet scent. She was too tempting and utterly dangerous to a man like him and yet...

Throwing caution to the wind, he grasped her tiny wrists and forced her arms flush against the door. Her breaths quickened, and she swallowed nervously. "Wh-what are you doing?"

He didn't have that answer. Instead, he turned the question around on her. "What game are you playing?"

"Game? I'm not playing a game with you."

"No? What do you call this? You know how it works when a loan isn't repaid."

He stopped abruptly and wondered at the way she had forced this confrontation. It was all too neat. With the amount of money on the line, she had to have known this day was coming. When the money had been borrowed, her brother had agreed to the terms. The car would be repossessed and sold on the black market if the loan defaulted, and the insurance check for the theft would be split eighty-twenty in favor of Besian. That's the way it worked. So why show up at the garage now? Why make such a scene? Why hadn't she simply paid the damn loan since she was so fucking rich?

Unless...

A prickly sensation invaded his stomach. "Is this a setup?"

Her honey brown eyes flashed with fear. "What? No!"

Not convinced by her denial, he quickly replayed their conversation so far. Had he said anything truly incriminating? Wondering if she was wearing a wire, he eyed her clothing. She seemed overdressed in that skirt and top with the pinkish red jacket, especially compared to her friend who wore a camisole and yoga pants. Her blonde hair was pulled up in a ponytail that looked purposely messy. Turquoise earrings dangled from her ears. She looked too pretty and too enticing.

Realizing he had been caught in her trap, he let go of her wrists and gave her jacket a shake. "Take this off. *Nou.*"

She pressed back against the door, moving as far away from him as possible. He took her retreat as confirmation of her duplicity. "No!"

"Yes." He started to push the jacket off her shoulders, intent on finding the wires, but she blindsided him with a well-placed smack that nearly took his head clean off his shoulders. Stunned by the power behind her slap, he blinked a few times before turning to face her.

Aston had gone ghostly pale. She seemed just as surprised that she had actually hit him. The fear etched into her beautiful face was easy enough to read now. His gut twisted, and he loathed himself for causing such fear in a woman. Her lower lip wobbled precariously. **"I'm** sorry."

"Don't." He fixed her with an angry glare. "When you hit someone, own it." Then, because she seemed like the sort of girl who needed a lesson in the realities of the world, he added, "The next time you hit a man like that you better be prepared to keep on fighting or run."

She turned up her dainty little nose rather haughtily. Her defiance should have pissed him off, but-God help him-he found that being smacked by her and then sneered at only made him want to claim those pouty lips of hers even more.

"There won't be a next time. I don't make a habit of hanging around men who think they can put their hands on me like you did. I prefer a better class."

Her words stung him, but he snorted derisively, pretending she hadn't hit her mark. "Next time borrow your money from a better class."

"I told you! I didn't borrow any money. I don't *need* to borrow money."

"Your brother did, and he came to us."

Her lips parted but no sound followed. Confusion was plain on her face. She seemed to be considering something very carefully. Finally, she spoke. "You didn't steal the car. You repossessed it as collateral for a loan Calvin took from your boss."

Her betrayed expression convinced him he had misjudged the situation. "You didn't know?"

"Of course I didn't know!" She shot him a withering look. "That car means the world to me! If I had known that my stupid stepbrother had taken out a loan using Baby as collateral, I would have marched over to one of your boss' strip clubs and tossed a suitcase of money at him."

"You named the car Baby?" He tried not smirk, but it was too precious.

She sobered. "My father named her. Baby was his car. Now she's *mine.* Calvin had no right to use her as collateral."

"Well, he did, and he didn't make any of the payments. This is the price of going back on his word." It wasn't any of his business, but he had to ask. "Why didn't your brother come to you for the money he needed?"

"Stepbrother," she said icily. "He's my stepbrother. He's not my real family."

"Family is family." He thought of the people who loved him like a brother but shared none of his blood-Besian, Zee, Devil. If that was the way she saw her stepbrother, as someone unfit to be part of her family, no fucking wonder he had screwed her over by taking her car and using it as collateral in a loan he had probably never intended to pay.

"Family?" She scoffed with a harsh laugh. "Family doesn't push you down the stairs and break your arm on the morning your parents are getting married. Family doesn't roofie you, tie a bow around your neck and leave you in a pool house as a gift for a friend's birthday. Family doesn't miss your father's funeral to ransack your house for all the valuables that aren't nailed down."

Her eyes glittered with fury and hurt. For the first time in a long fucking time, Ben experienced the urge to comfort someone...to *care.* He shoved it down just as quickly as it appeared. He had cared once and only once. After his mother had wasted away in hospice, he had vowed he would never care again. He wasn't about to break that vow now.

"If you'll give me back the car, I'll pay whatever Calvin owes plus interest and any other fees your boss wants to tack onto the account."

"That's not my decision to make. I can't negotiate something like that."

"So let's go visit your boss-"

"He's out of town. He won't be back until next week."

"Well...then...," she trailed off as she considered her options. "What if I trade you Baby for another car from the collection? Or two cars? Hell, I'll give you three or four of them if that's what you want."

Ben thought that was more than fair, but it wasn't his job to make those decisions. "I'll have to call the boss."

"So call him." She gestured to the phone on his desk. "I'll go find Baby and keep her company."

"The car isn't here."

"Where is she?"

"That car went straight to the storage containers to wait for shipment."

She exhaled with apparent relief. "So you didn't chop it up?"

"Do I look stupid to you? I boosted that one myself, just to be sure it was handled properly."

"You know what that car is worth, right?"

"Yes." He waited to see if she would mention an amount. "What's wrong? You don't want to talk money? Is that gauche?"

"Look at you! Using those big words. The libraries in juvenile detention must have benefited from all those literacy fundraisers my stepmother used to host." She cast a daring glance his way. "Well? Isn't that how you want me to talk to you?"

"That's not-" He clenched his jaw together. "How did you know I was in juvie?"

Her face softened. "I didn't. I just-I'm sorry. I shouldn't have taken the bait."

Grudgingly, he said, "I shouldn't have been such a dick."

"I have a feeling you probably have a reason for your attitude toward me."

"Why would you say that?"

She shrugged. "My dad made a lot of money and a lot of enemies. You wouldn't be the first person to have a grudge against me for something I never did."

Her matter-of-fact statement left him feeling lower than dirt. He had judged her to be one thing but was having second thoughts. Maybe there was more to Aston McNeil than the vapid stories would have him believe. The glimpses he was getting were helping him paint a picture of a young woman who had been born into privilege but who had suffered regardless.

"Ben?"

He liked the way his name sounded coming from her sweet mouth. "Yes?"

"Why did you try to undress me?"

"To see if you were wearing a wire," he answered truthfully.

Her anxious gaze met his, but she stared unwaveringly at him while shrugging out of her jacket. Extending it on one finger, she offered it to him and he took it. His mouth went dry as she lifted the bottom of her striped top and revealed the sloping plane of her tanned belly. She bared her lacy bra to him, the sheer, pale pink teasing him and making him wonder if her nipples were that same shade.

Turning around, she showed him her back before spinning to face him again and letting her top fall. When she gripped the bottom of her skirt, she might as well have stomped the gas pedal controlling his heart. His pulse revved up like a throttled engine. Inch by tantalizing inch, she uncovered her thighs. It was a better striptease than he had ever seen in one of the clubs the family owned. Not even the highest paid dancers had made his cock throb like this.

She kept her gaze trained on his face, her mouth curved with a hint of a shy smile, and continued lifting her skirt. When he got his first glimpse of her panties, his dick leapt with utter fucking joy. Ben had never seen panties like these. No doubt they cost more than he spent on groceries for a month but damn! They were so fucking sexy. In that same soft shade of pink as her bra, they were sheer like a fine net. Two embroidered shells covered the area he wanted to see most.

He noticed the tops of her thighs were flushed now, her skin bright red and betraying her embarrassment. Or maybe it was her excitement, he thought after glancing at her pretty face. Her lips were parted on a pitched breath. He caught a peek at her soft, pink tongue and it made him think about even softer, pinker parts that he wanted to see.

"Do you trust me now?" She held her skirt up high, still showing off her skimpy panties.

"I'm getting there." He made a sudden decision, one that he would probably come to regret. "The boss will have the final say on the debt, but since he's out of town, there's a good chance your car-your Baby-will be gone by the time he gets back. So I'll get your car back to you tonight and deal with the fallout from my boss-on onecondition."

"Anything," she said, her fingers clenching the fabric of her skirt even tighter.

Would she agree so quickly once she heard his terms? There was only one way to find out. "You belong to me for a week as collateral."

She blinked twice. "Belong to you? You mean...?"

Holding his breath, he nodded slowly. "You're mine for seven days and seven nights."

Aston stared at him for a long, tense moment. Her fingers straightened, and she dropped her skirt, smoothing out the fabric with deliberate sweeping motions. Taking a step toward him, she extended her hand and held his gaze. "Deal."

2 CHAPTER TWO

On trembling legs, I exited Ben's office and prayed Marley wouldn't be able to read the truth on my face. I spotted her leaning against the toolbox. Her eyes narrowed when she saw us. I joined her while Ben spoke to Devil in their shared language. I fought the urge to glance back at the tattooed mob enforcer who had just extracted the filthiest promise from me.

The wicked thrill of anticipation that raced through me left me feeling uncertain and confused. Why wasn't I ashamed? Why wasn't I disgusted with myself for trading my body for a car?

Long ago, my father had taught me the art of negotiation. *Know when you 're beat,* he had warned. *Get out early. Sell first. Close the deal.*

That's what I had done in the office. I couldn't take the chance that Ben's boss might take days to answer my request. The clock was already running. If I wanted Baby back, I had to make hard choices.

Not that it had been that hard of a choice, I silently acknowledged. When he had pinned me to that door, I had damn near fainted. Slapping him had been a dangerous move, but deep down, I had known he wouldn't hurt me. He seemed to enjoy pushing me though, scaring me as if to remind me that he wasn't like the men of my social circles. He had asked if I was playing a game, but he seemed to be the one playing with me.

"Well?" Marley tugged on my hand and turned her back to shield us as we talked with heads close together. "What did he say?"

"He said yes."

She looked unconvinced. "Just like that?"

"Sort of," I said, unwilling to lie totally to my best friend.

"Sort of?" Marley repeated. Her eyes widened slightly as she chanced a quick peek at Ben and caught sight of the bright red mark on his cheek. Judging by the amused glances from the men, she wasn't the only one who could see the faint outline of my fingers on his skin. Lowering her voice, she whispered, "Did you smack him?"

I had the decency to look apologetic. "Yes."

"Do I want to know why?"

"Probably not." I swallowed and glanced over my shoulder to see Ben waiting for me to finish up and follow him. "I have to go. He's taking me to get Baby. I'll call you when I get home."

"Be careful, Aston. Ben might let you get away with hitting him but the rest of this crew? Don't push your luck. Be smart. Get your car. Get the hell away from these guys."

I took her warning to heart. "I'll call you when I'm home."

"If anything happens-"

"I'll call you."

Reluctantly, she let go of my hand. Ben held my gaze for a moment before pivoting on his heel and striding toward a rear exit. His aloof treatment aggravated me but still I trailed after him like a stupid little puppy running after her master. For a girl who had gotten used to always being in control, there was something oddly intriguing about the way Ben didn't defer to me. I didn't like it, exactly, but I didn't hate it either.

I grimaced at the mugginess of the hot August night that greeted me, but Ben mistook the look for distaste at the mode of transportation he now offered.

Shoving his helmet toward me, he growled, "I'm sorry if the lady doesn't approve of the bike, but not all of us have the luxury of car collections worth millions of dollars and a different ride for each day of the week."

"For your information, I drive the same freaking Jeep every day." I snatched the helmet and fought the mounting desire to smack him with it. "I wasn't making a face because of your motorcycle. I was making a face because of this awful wet heat."

"Yeah. Sure you were." He jerked the helmet out of my hands and pressed it onto my head. I held perfectly still as he carefully guided it into place, making sure not to catch my earrings or my hair. He tightened the chin strap before buckling it into place. His tattooed knuckles brushed my skin and an arc of delicious anticipation burned through me.

Suddenly, I couldn't stop thinking about his rough hands lingering on other parts of me. For a moment, I thought he might be imagining the same thing. His hands had gone still, and he peered down at me with utter confusion reflected in his pale eyes. Then realization dawned. He didn't know what he was doing with me. He wanted to dislike me but he was helping me. He was breaking some rule and he didn't know why.

Grunting, he dropped his hands. A second later, he snatched my cell phone from my fingers, shoved it into his back pocket where it would be safe during the ride and turned toward his bike. I didn't know much about motorcycles. My father had always referred to them as two-wheeled deathtraps and had forbidden me from ever getting on one. Ben's bike wasn't flashy like the ones I had seen at car and bike shows over the years. It was the perfect combination of staid black with gleaming chrome, powerful and intimidating.

He carelessly slung his leg over the seat, and I couldn't stop staring at the taut denim stretched across his perfect backside. My gaze traveled along the beautifully violent swaths of tattoos running from his fingers to his shoulders and disappearing under his shirt. God, how I wanted to know where those tattoos ended. His chest? His belly? His legs?

Standing behind him, I could now see the massive double-headed eagle inked onto his back. The monstrous and intimidating sigil was easily visible through the thin white fabric of his sleeveless, tight tank. I had always found these so-called wife-beater shirts disgusting but not on Ben. It made him look sexy and dangerous.

"You plan on standing there all night?" He glanced back at me with irritation. His mouth pursed with unhappiness as he took in my bare legs. "Next time you ride with me, you'll wear jeans."

A secret thrill coursed through me at the mention of a next time. Glad that I had chosen the fuller, looser skirt this morning instead of the pencil, I bared my thighs to his view for the second time in less than twenty minutes and climbed onto the motorcycle. The big, black beast roared to life beneath me. I tried to find a place to put my feet but couldn't find a natural spot.

As if sensing my uncertainty, Ben reached down and clasped my ankle. He dragged my right foot into the right position, resting the toes of my pumps on a shiny peg before reaching down on the left side to do the same. Before I had a chance to get comfortable, he grabbed my hands and tugged them forward, pulling my arms around his waist. His fingertips grazed the back of my hand and trailed a line to my elbow before doubling back again. His feather-light touch awakened my entire body. The very core of me hummed with need.

Forced to lean forward, I pressed my cheek to his back. That masculine scent of him intoxicated me. I closed my eyes and enjoyed the vibrations of the bike as he eased out of the parking lot and onto the closest street. Holding onto this mysterious man and feeling the rush of wind against my bare skin, I finally understood why my father had forbidden me from riding on a motorcycle. He hadn't been afraid that I would be hurt by the bike. No, he had been afraid of the men who liked to ride them. They were far, far more hazardous to his baby girl than the two wheels and chrome they sat upon.

Opening my eyes, I enjoyed the whir of vehicles, lights and buildings flashing before me. Ben drove fast, but I had a feeling he was using more caution than usual with the added cargo clinging to his back. A strange feeling, one suspiciously akin to jealousy, speared me as I wondered how many other women had sat on this seat and held onto him as I did now. It was an irrational, weak thought that I detested almost immediately.

Yet I couldn't stop thinking about it. Ben Beciraj, with his strong arms and handsome face and that dangerous glint in his eyes, probably had women falling all over him. Marley had told me about the Albanian crime family and their business interests around Houston. Stealing cars and loan sharking were the tip of the iceberg for this crew. They also dealt in escorts and strip clubs. Surely Ben had his pick of those long-legged, curvy beauties who danced for money on the stages of the clubs owned by his boss. The image of

Ben finding pleasure with a gorgeous, lithe dancer twisted my stomach.

Stop it! Remember who he is. Remember what *he is. Remember what he made you promise!*

But even thinking of the promise he had extracted from me didn't make me want him any less. That was a far more maddening discovery.

We flew down the freeway until the bright flares and white plumes of smoke from the refineries came into view. He turned down a dimly lit street and eased off the throttle. The rumbling purr of the engine ricocheted off the seemingly endless rows of storage containers that surrounded us. This close to the refineries and the waterways of the port I wasn't surprised by the abundance of storage facilities. For all I knew, my father's holding company-my holding company now, I gently reminded myself-owned part or all of some of them.

He turned down a row of containers, drove three-quarters of the way down, and rolled to a stop. He killed the engine and reached back to pat my hip. I understood the silent instruction and climbed off of the bike first. My inner thighs were still vibrating and my legs were warm from the heat of the engine and exhaust. The night air, though muggy and hot, felt cool against my chest without the added heat of Ben's body pressed against mine.

Smoothly rising from his bike, Ben turned toward me and reached for the strap on my helmet. Just as carefully as before, he took away the helmet and placed it on the seat. My nose twitched at the sulfurous scent that surrounded us.

"What's wrong, sugar? Does the smell remind you of poor, working class people?"

Deciding I had had enough of his bitter remarks, I punched his upper arm. He actually smirked at my attack, probably because my fist bounced off his steely muscles like a child's might. He caught my fist before I could yank it back, but his grip wasn't cruel. "You planning on hitting me again or running?"

"Depends on whether you intend to cut the asshole act or not," I answered bravely. "There's no one here you need to impress with the hard ass routine. It's just us. Just you and me."

His smirk faltered, and he let go of my hand. Glancing away from me, he fished a key ring out of his pocket. He gestured to a container near the end of the row. I walked beside him in silence for a few seconds. "Money," I said eventually. "It's the smell of money."

He cast an amused glance my way. "Oh, is that what it is?"

"That's what Daddy called it. It's the smell of opportunity."

"For people like you? Yes. For people like me? Not so much."

I rolled my eyes and let it go. Twenty plus years had etched that chip into his shoulder. There was no way I could buff it out in the short time we were going to spend together.

Out of necessity, I silently added. *I'm only with him because I have to be.*

But that wasn't really true, was it?

"You were close to your father?" He sounded genuinely interested.

"Yes. After my mom..." My voice faded as I tried to find the nicest way to put that story. "After my mom...died, he took me out of private school and had me tutored at home. He would drag me from one business meeting to another. Before I knew it, I was sitting in the corner of his office every day, doing my math homework and listening to conversations about arbitrage and financial instruments."

"He was grooming you to takeover someday." Ben stopped in front of the container and flicked through his keys until he found the right one. "You're lucky that he loved you so much. A lot of kids aren't that lucky."

Did he count himself among the unlucky? I wanted to ask about his parents but something about the hard set to his jaw warned me not to do it.

He jammed the key into the padlock and gave it a twist. After removing the lock, he shoved down the levered handle of the door and started to push the heavy slab of metal to the left. "Well, here's your Baby."

But she wasn't there.

Ben's stomach dropped when he realized the container was empty. He shoved the door all the way open and stormed into the oversized metal box. Dread gripped his gut. Swearing up a storm in English and Albanian, he rushed out of the container and straight over to the one across from it. He found the right key and made quick work of unlocking the door.

When he shoved the door aside, he discovered the Ferrari that should have been there was missing too. His stomach clenching, he moved to the container to the left and the one on the right, finding them all empty. The fifth and final container he searched was the only one that held a car. He let out a relieved sigh upon finding the '69 Chevy Camara.

"Ben?" Aston's soft voice interrupted his racing thoughts.

"Not now," he growled unkindly while digging his phone from his pocket. He should apologize for his rudeness to her, but he had a bad feeling about the missing vehicles. This was the sort of thing that got men killed. He had been the last man here. Was he followed? Who had the balls to rob the Albanian fucking mafia?

He pinched the bridge of his nose while he waited for Besian to answer. He mentally calculated the time difference. It was very early morning in Tirana. What a fucking wakeup call the boss was about to receive!

"Someone had better be dying," Besian snarled, his voice husky from sleep. He was still recovering from the bullet wound that had nearly killed him. Although he waved off everyone's concern, Ben knew him too well. Besian was hurting and struggling to get enough rest. His responsibilities weren't making it easy for him to recuperate.

"I'm at the holding pens. The cars we boosted tonight are gone."

"Gone." Ben heard the rustle of sheets and a hiss of pain. "What do you mean they're gone?"

Not wanting to get into the side deal he had made with Aston, he chose to lie. "I lost my phone and thought I might have left it in the last car I parked in the containers. Nothing looks disturbed. The locks weren't cut or broken."

"But the cars are gone?"

"All but the Camara."

"Did Zee give you a pickup time?"

"Tomorrow night," he answered and checked his watch. "He's probably just getting close to US airspace now. When I spoke to him while he was in Dubai, he said he would arrive around three this morning. He would have called me if he wanted to move up the timetable."

Besian made an angry sound. "I need to make some calls. It could be someone from the outside, but if the locks weren't broken..."

"Yes." He hated to think one of their own men would betray them. He shuddered to think what Besian would do if the culprit came from their own ranks. It would be bloody and brutal and the sort of work Devil relished.

"Look, if it's the cartel coming back on us for all that shit that went down with Abby Kirkwood and Jack Connolly, I want you to stay out of it. There's enough bloodshed going on in Mexico. We don't need it here. I've already spoken to Lalo about the contracts we had with him. We've settled it, and we're done."

It was the one point of business Ben didn't agree with and the only time he had dared to argue with Besian. Lalo Contreras, the one-time low-level enforcer and now kingpin, was good for business. He always needed modified cars for his dealers, and Ben excelled in building traps, the hidey holes the dealers used for stowing drugs, money and guns. When Besian had cut off that business, he had cut Ben's earnings in half. It wasn't an easy thing to swallow, but he had choked it down because that was the decision the boss had made. His loyalty wouldn't allow him to do anything else.

"Listen, I want you to--"

"Ben?" Aston whispered urgently. "I think-"

He cut her off with a wave of his hand and prayed the boss hadn't heard her in the background. Apparently he hadn't because he kept talking and laying out his plan.

"Ben!" She was slightly louder this time but still he didn't turn around. Instead he tried to pay close attention to his orders.

"Right. Okay. I'll get it done."

"Good. Call me if anything changes."

"Yeah." His phone was still pressed to his ear when Aston planted both hands against his back and shoved him forward. He lost his balance and tumbled onto the hood of the Camara. Whirling around and braced for an attack, he spotted a flash of blonde hair as she leapt into the container with him.

"Help me! Hurry! They're coming!"

"What?" He didn't wait for her answer. He rushed to her side and hurriedly shut the door, leaving only a small crack so he could see. "Who?"

"I don't know." She clutched onto his arm. He was surprised that he didn't have the slightest inclination to shake her off. Instead, he slid his arm around her shoulders and dragged her closer. "I walked to the other end of the container while you were talking. I thought maybe I might find something. Tire treads or whatever," she explained. "I saw two SUVs and panicked. What if the people who stole Baby are back for this one?"

"If it's them, we need to get out of here." She was a liability. She had no weapon and no fighting experience. If anything happened to her, there would be too much heat and attention turned onto the family. Besian really would have his balls if they ended up on the front page of the newspaper.

Glancing back at the Camara, he decided that running was their best option. His bike would leave her too exposed. He angled his face and peered through the small slit he had left open to see the SUVs coming closer. There wouldn't be much time to do it right.

"Get in the driver's seat. The keys are in the ignition. We'll only have a few seconds," he warned, already putting his weight against the door.

He expected her to protest but she ran to the driver's seat, managed to get the door open wide enough to slip inside and started the classic muscle car. The second the engine purred to life, he threw open the door and turned back to see her rolling down the passenger side window. He jumped out of the container, giving her plenty of room to spin out of the box and jumped back when the car hit the ground. Grabbing the roof, he swung his legs through the window and wriggled through it as she punched the gas hard enough to throw him into the dash.

"You should probably put on your seatbelt," she warned, slamming the gas pedal even harder.

"No shit," he grunted while bracing his boot against the dash. Reaching down, he jerked free his backup weapon, cursing his mistake of leaving his favored one locked in his desk, and twisted in his seat to see if they were being followed. He turned just in time to see the lead SUV slam into his motorcycle. The impact tossed the bike into the air and into the closest container. His anger soared, but he didn't have time for plotting his revenge. A young kid, maybe twenty-one, armed with an automatic weapon leaned out a window.

"Keep your head down!" He put his hand on her soft blonde hair and applied pressure. "Keep driving."

The first gunshot missed the car but the second, third and fourth ricocheted off the trunk and roof of the Camara. Praying that she wouldn't wreck, he fired back at the SUV in the lead. He was careful with his shots and mindful of his short supply of ammunition. Instead of trying for the tires or the engine block, he aimed at the driver, contorting his body into a position that put him at high risk of being hit to get the best shot.

Three rounds fired-and the final hit its mark. The SUV careened into a container and crumpled. The vehicle following it clipped the rear end of the wrecked SUV but didn't stop. He started to fire again to stop the second SUV, but Aston gripped his shirt, her fingernails scratching his stomach. "Hold on!"

He had only a moment to react. He slid back down into his seat just in time to see her take a turn that most stunt drivers couldn't make. Her pretty little foot, encased in that outrageously expensive high heel, moved expertly between the clutch and the gas and ghosted over the brake while her hand worked the gear shift without hesitation. He wasn't sure whether he should be terrified his life was in her hands or aroused by how damned sexy she was behind the wheel.

She barreled down a side street and made another wicked turn that almost sent him flying out the window. Remembering her earlier comment about the seatbelt, he grabbed the thin strap and hurriedly jammed the latch into place. The lap belt wouldn't be much use in a head-on collision but it was better than nothing.

With her lips pursed and her jaw tight, Aston put more distance between them and the SUV trying to catch up. She hooked another wicked right, but he was ready for this one and had his hand on the door panel to stay in place. He wasn't sure how the hell she managed to stay in her seat-or how she managed to look so fucking hot doing it. Something told him Jack McNeil had taught his daughter more than just business tactics.

The SUV chasing them misjudged the turn and lost control. It hit the corner of an abandoned building and would drive no farther tonight. She didn't slow down though. Punching the gas, she tore down the street like a bat out of hell and didn't ease up until she hit the 225.

As if overcome by the adrenaline, she started to giggle. The sound made his lips twitch with amusement. Her childish giggles morphed into throaty belly laughter. She tossed her head back-and he felt himself teetering on the precipice and in real danger of falling.

He didn't think he had ever seen anything so beautiful as Aston McNeil laughing, her cheeks flushed with adrenaline and her eyes sparkling with relief. She held out a trembling hand. "Look at me! I'm shaking."

Unable to help himself, he reached for her hand. The spark of contact made her inhale sharply. He interlaced their fingers and grinned at her. "You crazy, beautiful girl!"

She snorted in the most unladylike way but didn't drop his hand. With fingers entwined, she lowered their joined hands to the gear shift. "We can't go back to your garage."

"No," he agreed. "And we can't go back to your place or mine. They'll have recognized me, and if this was an inside job, they'll know you're with me." Considering their precarious position, he added, "We have to stay off the main highways. This car has probably been reported as stolen so keep it under the speed limit and be careful."

She shot him a look that said she could charm her way out of even a situation as severe as being pulled over in a stolen car. He would like to think that she wouldn't turn on him, maybe even call him a kidnapper or worse, but his childhood had taught him to be wary.

"Where are we going, Ben?"

He had a place in mind, but she wasn't going to like it.

3 CHAPTER THREE

A brothel. He brought me to a brothel!

"Quit staring," Ben hissed. Taking my hand, he tugged me along beside him. "And keep your head down. You might see someone you recognize."

The thought of it mortified me. I tried to follow his instructions but couldn't quell my raging curiosity. I would never set foot in a place like this again so I might as well gawk. He was right, though. I did see someone I noticed. The familiar face of a federal judge who used to play golf with my father stunned me. Ben must have felt my shock because he pulled me tight against him and angled his body to block my view and keep my face hidden from others.

I hurried to match his steps as he led me upstairs and to a room near the end of the right hall. He unlocked the door and pushed me inside before locking the door behind us. A lamp burned in the corner of the lavishly decorated boudoir. Like the rest of the historic home tucked away in one of the old, quiet neighborhoods of the city, the bedroom showcased beautiful antique furnishing and rich colors.

Turning to face Ben, I noted the way he leaned against the door. He seemed tense and ready for a fight. I didn't feel like giving him one. Curious about how he knew about this high-end brothel, I asked the obvious question, "So...um...do you come here a lot?"

He shot me a warning look. "I don't have to pay for pussy."

His crass reply rendered me speechless. He glanced away from me and shoved off the door. His next words shocked me even more than the last ones. "I was born here. My mother was one of the most famous prostitutes this town has ever known."

My lips parted, but I couldn't think of anything smart to say. Suddenly that chip on his shoulder made sense. How many wealthy men had pawed at his mother? Was his own dad a member of my exclusive social circle? Was he a bastard son that had been shut out of his rich father's life?

Following Ben's slow movement around the room, I decided to keep my mouth shut and let him say whatever he needed to say. If he didn't want to say anything that was okay, too.

"My father was one of her customers." He toyed with a porcelain figurine on a side table. "He was Besian's old boss. Not Afrim Barisha," he clarified, as if I should know who that was, "but the man before him, Baki Beciraj. He let me have his name, but he didn't want me, and I let that rage twist me up. I got into trouble. I did stupid things. Then, one day, Besian saved me."

"Your boss now?"

He nodded, still refusing to make eye contact with me. "He adopted me as his nephew and made it possible for me to be recognized as part of the family."

I understood that he wasn't talking his father's blood family but the crime family he now served. "And your mother?"

"She died when I was twenty." He finally looked at me. "Ovarian cancer. She didn't even realize she had it until it was too late." He pushed the figurine across the table as a silence settled between us. "So are you disgusted now?"

"No. Why would I be?"

"I'm the son of a whore and a mob boss."

Hating to hear such self-loathing in his voice, I asked the only question that mattered. "Did you love your mother?"

"Yes." He didn't even hesitate.

"Did she love you?"

"Yes."

"Then none of that other stuff matters."

He made a scoffing noise. "You wouldn't understand. You've had a perfect life with-"

"My mother was a drug addict," I cut in quickly. "Daddy said that she had always been a little too fond of partying, but he thought she would settle down once they were married. She, uh, she lost her first two babies-boys-because of the cocaine. Daddy forced her into a rehab after the second stillbirth."

His hard glare softened. "Jesus. Did she stay clean?"

"For a while, until I was born," I answered. "I got sick when I was four months old, and Daddy found out that she had been using again and breastfeeding me. He...wasn't happy."

"I can imagine."

"While I was in the hospital going through baby coke withdrawal, he sent her away. He put her in another house in a different state and told her that she couldn't come back unless she got clean and stayed clean for an entire year."

"Did she?"

I nodded. "She came back when I was two. I don't remember, of course, but I've seen pictures of her homecoming. We were happy for a while."

"Until?"

"She started having an affair with her trainer. He took her to a party, and she started using again. Pills this time," I added. "I was too young to understand why she was sleeping during the day and so wired at night. She started drinking too much. Sometimes even when we she picked me up from school..."

The ugly memories twisted my gut and left me sick inside. I rubbed the back of my neck with cold, clammy hands. "She was bringing me home from a ballet recital. Daddy had been kept away on business. He was stuck in an airport somewhere, and Mom...she had been popping pills and drinking before the recital."

"What happened?" He asked the question as if he already knew the answer.

"She was too drunk and stoned to follow the signs in a construction zone. She got onto the interstate driving the wrong way, and she was weaving all over the place before she finally passed out. I was screaming. I was so scared-and then she slammed into a concrete barrier. I don't...! don't remember anything after that."

"She died?"

I nodded.

"And you lived."

I nodded again and met his hard gaze. "So, you see, Ben, we're not so different. We both had parents who were less than ideal, but we've turned out okay."

He crossed the distance between us in two long strides and placed his hand against my cheek. My eyelids drifted together as his callused fingers glided over my skin. "Not so different," he agreed, "but not so much alike either."

"That makes things interesting." Finding some courage, I rose on tiptoes and pressed my lips to his. His hands flew to my shoulders, and for a moment, I thought he was going to shove me away from him. Instead, he pulled me even closer. His powerful arms engulfed me as he groaned against my mouth, the sound so very hungry and needful. He picked me up, and I wrapped my legs around his waist.

We were playing with fire. We'd known each other for an hour and already we were locking lips. Of course, we had just survived being chased and shot at by criminals.

And now you're being kissed by a criminal.

The truth was painful and raw-but it was real. Ben wasn't a lawyer or a doctor. He wasn't a professional athlete or a banker. He was a mechanic, a mob enforcer and a car thief.

And he could kiss.

My God, could he kiss!

Lightheaded and trembling, I clutched at his shoulders as he stabbed his tongue between my lips. He bit my lower lip with enough pressure to make me gasp. I had a feeling he had done it to remind me that he wasn't a nice man and that he could hurt me--that he *would* hurt me.

Refusing to be cowed, I cupped the back of his head and deepened our kiss, wresting control from him and proving I could give as well he gave. Ben turned around and put a knee on the bed, taking me down to the mattress. He broke away from my mouth just long enough to hitch me up a little higher on the bed and throw his legs on the outside of mine. Then he was attacking my mouth again and driving me crazy with his wicked tongue.

"Aston?"

"Yes?"

"You're out of college, right?"

"I'm in grad school." I pulled back and peered up at him. "Why?"

He brushed his knuckles across my cheek. "You look young. I wanted to be sure."

I rolled my eyes. "I'm not a card-carrying member of the V Club, either, if that's on your list. You aren't taking advantage of me."

"I am." His gaze turned dark. "I made you trade your body for your car."

"Nobody makes me do anything. Not you, not my father, not my evil stepbrother. I make my own choic-es. *Always."*

At the mention of Calvin, he jerked back his hand. "Aston, earlier, you said that he drugged you and gave you to his friend. Did that friend-did he hurt you?" He swallowed. "I don't want to scare you. I don't want to hurt you more."

His concern touched me. Considering that he had probably spent his formative years running the halls of this very brothel, I could only imagine the awful things he might have seen. To know that he wanted to spare me any trauma endeared him to me.

Running my fingers through his hair, I told him what he wanted to know. "Russ didn't hurt me. He had the biggest crush on me, and I guess Calvin had been sending him these fake love letters and emails. It was really sick how far he was willing to go to set it up, but he failed. When Russ realized I had been roofied, he got me dressed and drove me straight to

the nearest hotel to sober up. Later, he called my father and told him everything."

"How old were you?"

"Sixteen," I said, remembering how humiliating and devastating the experience had been. "Marley wanted to tell Spider. She swore he would gut Calvin for doing something so cruel."

"He would have done worse. What about your father? What did he do?"

I closed my eyes as the violent memories returned. "I had never seen him that angry. I thought he really was going to kill Calvin. He beat him to a bloody pulp in the foyer of the house. Just beat the shit out of him until our housekeeper and her husband finally intervened and dragged him off. Calvin laughed. He had blood running down his face, and he couldn't stop laughing."

"What about Calvin's mother? Did she say anything?"

"Marjorie? I think she knew he was...broken. She was afraid of him just like me. When she died from an allergic reaction a few years later, we found a letter with her will that warned Daddy to be careful because Calvin wasn't stable. She said that she had always feared he was going to kill her or me."

Ben clasped my chin and stared at me. "I won't let him hurt you."

Running my hands along Ben's strong arms, I said, "You might actually be the only person in the whole world who can keep that promise."

Something in Ben's demeanor changed. Instead of the rough, quick fuck I had been expecting, he treated me gently. I sensed he was trying to make a point. Shivering with excitement, I reveled in the way his powerful hands moved over my body. He stripped me easily, shifting me this way and that to tug free my clothing until I was naked underneath him.

Wanting to feel his skin on mine, I grasped the bottom of his shirt. He sat up and finished taking it off himself, kicking off his boots and peeling away his socks while he was at it. His jeans and boxers followed and then he was on top of me.

He kissed me with such tenderness and took his time making love to my mouth. Our tongues dueled, his winning the fight and leaving me breathless. I clenched my thighs together as a pulsing heat throbbed there. My nipples were tight, pulsing peaks by now.

Ben soothed the ache in my breasts with his hands and mouth. He massaged my supple flesh and suckled me with long, hard tugs. Each sucking pull on my nipple traveled right down to my clitoris. The swollen little nub wanted to be played with, but Ben was busy with my breasts. I squeezed my thighs together again and drew his attention.

With a wolfish grin that made my insides wobble, Ben kissed his way down my body. He took his time on the downward trek, meandering around my belly and along my hips before ending up at my thighs. He slid to his knees next to the bed, and I realized he was going to do *that.*

"Do you like having your cunt licked?"

I made a choking sound that teetered on the verge of indignant but was really more shocked than anything.

"Oh, right. I guess that *better class* of men you prefer doesn't use words like cunt."

"Ben," I said warningly, my face on fire now. "Don't be so crude."

"I'll be whatever the hell I like." He parted my thighs with his strong hands and kneaded my sensitive flesh. He nibbled and nipped at my inner legs. I gasped and squirmed, but he didn't stop. "You never answered me. Do you like having your pussy eaten?"

"I..." Gulping nervously, I admitted, "It's not something I've experienced much. I think I like it."

"You think?" He made a *humph* sound. "Sounds like the men you've let into your bed don't know what they're doing. A sweet, pink pussy like this one?" He parted me with his thumbs and made a hungry noise that caused me to blush. "I know what to do with it."

Without warning, he swiped his tongue along my slit. I exhaled roughly and gripped the duvet beneath me. He repeated the motion twice before probing between my labia and finding my clit. As if savoring his favorite dessert, Ben took his sweet time between my thighs.

He slipped a finger inside my pussy, working it in and out of me at a leisurely pace. His tongue was the real star of the show. He did such sinful things with it, things that made me squeal and things that made me groan. He lapped at my clit and sucked on the little bud before fluttering his tongue over it.

"Ben!" He chuckled against my clit, and the low, rumbling vibrations felt so wickedly good. Finding the perfect rhythm, he licked and suckled until my hips shot off the bed. Rocked with spasms, I surfed the blissful waves gripping my lower belly. "Ben!"

Growling like a damned bear, he grabbed my bottom with his free hand and held me fast to his mouth, refusing to allow my escape as he drew out my climax. Only when I was limp and whimpering did he let go of me. By then, I was too boneless to move. His tongue continued to roam my pussy, sliding through my folds and even replacing his finger. I found it hard to breathe as he explored and tormented me, but I didn't want him to stop.

When he finally dragged his mouth away from me and stood, I caught sight of his shaft. I sat up and eyed the impressive cock jutting out from a thick thatch of dark hair. With an enthusiastic smile, I replaced his hand with mine and fondled his heavy length. I stroked up and down his erection, swirling my hand and marveling at the velvety steel beneath my fingers.

Wanting to taste him, I moved to a kneeling position. Ben seemed uncertain when I glanced up at him. His hesitance surprised me. "Aston, you don't have to--"

"Shut up, and let me suck your cock."

My brash reply stunned him, and he laughed. Before he could recover from hearing me using the coarse language he seemed to love, I painted the tip of him with my tongue. **His** laughter transformed to a groan, the noisy, needful sound exciting me and encouraging my exploration. I licked my lips, wetting them nicely, and then wrapped them around his cock.

"Fuck yes," he growled. "God, your mouth is so hot."

Thrilled by his reaction, I tried to make the experience good for him. I took him deeper and deeper with every downward stroke of my mouth. For a moment, I thought he might be disappointed that he couldn't bury himself in the back of my throat, but he didn't seem to mind in the least. His threaded his fingers into my hair, making a mess of my artfully arranged ponytail, and gently pumped his hips. Our gazes met, his needy and dark, and I saw that he wasn't going to try to wrest control from me. I could go as fast or as slow, as shallow or deep, as I wanted.

Wrapping my hand around the bottom of his shaft, I bobbed on the crown of his cock. I used my tongue in the way that seemed to make him breathe the hardest, rubbing it along the sensitive underside of his head. He wasn't the only one breathing hard, and I wasn't panting from exertion either. I was getting hot again.

Ben gently moved aside my hand and grasped his shaft. Realizing he was close and wanted to be in control now, I sat back on my heels and placed my hands against his thighs. His muscles bunched and tensed under my hands. Nostrils flaring and cheek twitching, he said, "Touch your tits. Pinch your nipples for me."

No one had ever dared to give me such an order. I should have been outraged that he thought he could order me around like a sex doll, but I couldn't ignore the way it made me breathless and lightheaded. When I pinched my nipples, the bright bite of pain caused my clit to throb mercilessly. I liked it. I liked it a lot.

"Open your mouth. Tongue out," he added, stroking faster now. When I complied, he smiled down at me, his eyes shining with approval. "That's it. Just. Like. That."

With a groan that erupted from deep inside him, Ben climaxed. His hot cum splashed my tongue, the white bursts of it pooling there. I didn't break eye contact with him, not even once, and that seemed to make him come even harder. He milked the last drops onto my tongue before sweetly caressing my face. I swallowed his seed, my mouth curving with pleasure when he used his thumb to swipe me clean.

Somehow he knew that I was aroused again. With one swift movement, he picked me up and tossed me onto the bed. He climbed up beside me, trapping one of my legs under his and forcing my thighs open again. He gazed at my sex and probed me with his thick, rough fingers. "Look at how shiny and wet your pussy is, baby. Does sucking cock turn you on?"

"Yes." There was no point in denying what he could see.

"Do you want me to make you come again?"

I rocked my hips and bit my lower lip. "Yes."

Two fingers speared me and his thumb flicked side to side over the engorged bud that ached ceaselessly. Ben kissed me like a starving man, his tongue stabbing against mine again and again. Lost in the sensations he evoked, I climaxed quickly. Thrashing atop the bed, I relished the powerful release he gave me and sagged against him when it was all over.

He ran his finger along my lower belly and drew shapes on my skin. His initials maybe? The thought of him branding me as his after only one time together should have perturbed me, but I found the possessive gesture exhilarating. What mark would he choose for me? It would be a beautiful tattoo I was sure but nothing so simple as his initials or his name.

Exhaling loudly, he finally spoke. "I have to leave for a while. I'll be back before sunrise, but you need to stay here."

"I can't hide out here indefinitely, Ben. I'm not the CEO yet but I'm working hard to earn my place while studying for my MBA. It's all right if I miss one day, but..."

"I'll have you back in your office by Monday." Ben hovered over me and traced his thumb along my lower lip. "I'll get Baby back too."

The mention of the prized car that Calvin had stupidly given away made my heart ache. "I think she's gone forever. There's no way we'll ever find her again."

He smiled before teasing his mouth against mine. "You don't know the people I know. There's nothing we can't find."

He kissed me properly now, our tongues flicking together and lingering. His forehead touched mine. "Stay here. Open that door for no one but me. Understand?"

"Yes."

"Good girl." He said it in such an endearing way that I could only smile.

Rolling onto my side, I watched him dress and enjoyed the view of his magnificently toned and inked body. I couldn't wait to have him again and was already planning the ways I wanted him to take me. He wouldn't make me feel bad for asking for the things I really wanted in bed-a smack on the bottom, a yank of my hair, a nip on my shoulder. Thinking of the aggressive way he had taken me just now, I wondered if I would even have to ask.

"You keep staring at me like that and I'm going to have to pin you to that mattress again." He jammed his foot into his boot. "But it won't be my fingers or my tongue enjoying your cunt this time."

"Ben!" My face flamed with embarrassment. "You can't say things like that!"

"I can, and I will." Amused by my scandalized expression, he leaned down and kissed me long and hard and deep. He palmed my breast and pinched my nipple between his fingers, not to hurt me but to make me tingle and ache in the very best way. Breaking off the kiss, he whispered, "Get some rest. I'll take care of this. I'll take care of you."

He spoke the words so easily. I tried to remember the last time a man had promised to take care of me. A memory of my father's last lucid moments in hospice flittered before me. Hating the sadness that threatened to overwhelm me, I pressed my lips to Ben's one last time. "Be safe. Please."

Surprise filtered across his face at my plea for his safety. "Don't worry about me. I'll have Devil with me. No one fucks with him."

Remembering the man's scarred face, I didn't doubt that. "What happened to his face?"

"Oh, sweetheart, that's not a story you want to hear before bed." He curled some of my hair around his finger and gave it a tug. "I'll be back soon. Lock the door behind me."

I shadowed him to the door. Before he stepped out into the hall, he seemed to remember something. Turning back to me, he retrieved my cell phone from his back pocket and then handed over the handgun he had just tucked into the waistband of his jeans. He held onto the muzzle and didn't let me take it right away. "Do you know how to use this?"

"This is Texas, Ben. I was shooting guns and going hunting at, like, six years old."

He released it into my hand. "Keep the safety on until you need it."

After pressing a lingering kiss to the crown of my head, he darted into the hall. I hid my naked body behind the door and turned the deadbolt as instructed. Sliding back into bed, I tried not to think about how many other naked couples had writhed with passion on this heavenly, plush mattress. I also didn't want to think about being shot at or my stupid stepbrother losing Baby or how much danger Ben was in at this very moment.

Closing my eyes, I chose instead to think about Ben and that sinful, wicked mouth of his.

4 CHAPTER FOUR

Ben spotted the quad cab truck idling at the end of the quiet street. He had left Madam Alina's brothel silently and without seeing anyone. Now he kept to the shadows, moving down the sidewalk with purpose. Always alert, he scanned his surroundings. After being shot at, he was jumpy and expecting another attack at any moment.

He tried to stay focused on the matter at hand, but his thoughts strayed back to Aston. For the first time in his life, he had actually been reluctant to leave a woman's bed. He had never wanted to linger or cuddle. That simply wasn't his way. He liked a good, hard fuck and a quick exit, but Aston with her swollen pink lips, bright eyes and soft hands made him want to stay. He wanted to take his time and explore her lush curves. More than anything, he wanted to show her pleasure like she had never known.

When he slid into the front passenger seat, Devil cast a knowing glance in his direction. Shaking his head, he put the truck in drive and pulled away from the curb. "You fucked her."

"No." It was the truth, but only technically.

"It's a bad idea."

"I know."

"So stop listening to your dick," Devil warned. "A girl like that? She's not for men like us. It won't end well."

It was a reminder he didn't need. "Did you go to the containers?"

Devil let the discussion shift without complaint. "Yes. Your bike is back at the shop, but it's fucked. We searched the SUV left at the storage center."

"And?"

"It belonged to the 1-8-7 crew. We found a bloody shoe with their gang sign all over it. Whispers has already heard that you clipped their leader. Another one ended up in the hospital."

The name of the startup street gang that had been trying to take over some of the territory their family controlled surprised him. "You're sure? They don't have any money. How are they buying weapons and vehicles?"

"They've got an anonymous backer."

"Who would back a bunch of punks? Half of them are barely out of high school."

"Which is why they're stupid enough to think they can steal from us," Devil interjected. "Do you think any other crew in this town would have the balls to do something so brazen?"

"Not unless they wanted a war," he said, "and there's already enough of a threat of that with all the cartel bullshit spilling into the city."

South of the border, the Guzman cartel was in the throes of an internal rebellion. So far, the bosses of Houston had been able to keep most of the mess away from the city limits, but Ben had a feeling the tenuous peace wouldn't last. Alliances were being forged, and only an idiot would take on their family who held one of the strongest positions of all.

"There's something else you should know." Devil glanced at him as they idled at a red light. "I asked around about the money the brother borrowed."

"Stepbrother," Ben corrected, thinking of the awful things that rat bastard had done to Aston.

"Whatever. Listen-the rumor is the brother borrowed the money from us to buy a large shipment from the cartel."

Now that was interesting. "Cocaine?"

"A mix, I heard. Coke, dope, weed-the kid bought a lot. He should have made a nice return on his investment, even after paying his dealers, the loan to us and the balance to the cartel,"

"But?" He sensed this story had a hell of a twist coming.

"The dumbass got robbed." Devil paused a moment, as if waiting for him to put the puzzle pieces together.

"By the 1-8-7 crew?"

"That's the rumor."

"Uh-huh." He crossed his arms and stretched out his long legs as far as they would go. "This was no coincidence. The same gang who ripped him off just happened to steal the car we repossessed from him? I don't buy it."

"You shouldn't. The stories I heard about the brother? He's a bad seed."

"I know. He hurt Aston. More than once," he added, certain the few instances she had told him were just the tip of the iceberg. "He thinks he's smart, playing all of us off each other. He borrows the money from us with no intention of paying it back and used a car that didn't belong to him to pay the balance so he wouldn't take the hit. Then he has his little asshole crew steal the cars from us. So now he has money, cars to sell *and* the drugs. But the cartel-Lalo's men-will tear this city up looking for the people who stole their product. He has no idea what he's done."

"If he does know, he doesn't care." Devil pointed to the glove box. "The rest of our men are waiting for us at the 1-8-7 headquarters. We'll knock them around and get our cars back."

"I suspect one of the boosters betrayed us." He found a clean piece and ammo waiting for him. "They knew which storage center we were using tonight, and they were the only ones we didn't have eyes on all night. They could have gotten keys made easily."

"I figured as much. I sent Karl and Peter to round them up and take them to the warehouse." A harsh laugh escaped Devil's throat. "They'll probably piss themselves when they see it."

Ben had seen harder men than the boosters do the same thing when faced with the place. The mention of the warehouse and the things that had been done there brought silence to the cab of the truck. He couldn't help but think about the young kids who were about to learn a painful lesson about the ugly underworld they had chosen to infiltrate. This wasn't a game. The sooner they learned the harsh realities, the better.

When they arrived at a rundown dance club, the parking lot was empty except for an SUV and two cars. They had passed three vehicles carrying their own men two blocks down the street. One of them went round to the front to block the entrance. The other two followed them into the lot so they could hit the upstart crew hard and fast from the rear.

At twenty-seven, Ben was younger than every other man in the crew, but they looked to him for guidance because he had earned his spot as *mik* for their crew by getting his hands dirty. He made a gesture that said not to kill anyone. There would be blood and pain, but he didn't want the mess of cleaning up anything worse on his hands-or his conscience.

When Devil used all seven feet of his beastly body to kick in the door, Ben heard Aston's voice urging him to be careful. Like a bunch of cockroaches hit with a beam of light, the twelve guys getting high and drinking after hours scattered across the club's main floor. There wasn't anywhere to run, of course, but that didn't stop them from trying. The pounding, thumping bass of hip hop music covered the clash of vicious fighting. For a band of street-wise punks, they were terrible fighters. Only one of them, the youngest one, got in any good licks. Seeing one of their own teetering on the edge of being shanked, Devil stepped over and slammed his massive fist into the face of that kid. The smaller body dropped to the ground.

Ben caught a familiar younger man by the back of his shirt and jerked him close. It was the kid who had tried to attack Abby Kirkwood, the pawn shop owner under the family's protection, over some stupid beef about gold chains. Later, he had thrown a brick through her front window. The boss had beat the shit out of the kid for daring to harm an innocent woman and had warned him not to stray across the territory lines again. Apparently the lesson hadn't taken hold. This time it would.

Half an hour later, the crew was trussed up with extension cords and ropes and piled together in the center of the dance floor. Someone finally turned down the music. Ben cleaned his bloodied knuckles on a bar towel Devil had slapped against his chest and crouched down to stare into the panicked eyes of the 1-8-7 kids.

And they were just kids. They were nineteen and twenty years old, too stupid to know better than to poke the hornet's nest but old enough to understand this night could only end one of two ways.

"So, which one of you assholes is in charge now?"

The kid who had tried to hurt Abby raised his bound hands. "Me."

"You?" Ben glanced around the room, but no one else volunteered for the position. "Okay." He reached out and dabbed at the trickle of blood running from the nose of the younger man he had caught. It was a comforting gesture meant to be disarming and unsettling. "Where are the cars?"

The kid swallowed hard before finally admitting, "We stashed them. They're sitting in a junk yard."

"All of them?"

The kid shook his head, the gold chains around his neck rattling. "I gave the James Bond car to Lalo Contreras as repayment for a debt."

"Calvin's debt?"

"Yes."

"What do you know about him?" The kid hesitated so Ben gripped the front of his shirt. "You know what will happen if you lie to me."

He gulped nervously. "He hired us to break into his house and steal all of the drugs he'd bought from Lalo. He put us in touch with a booster from your crew who told us where to find the cars tonight."

Ben glanced at Devil who still had blood drying on his hands before looking back at the kid. "Where's the shipment Calvin had you steal?"

"I've got it hidden some place safe. He's supposed to pick it up tomorrow night."

"Well, you're going to take me to it tonight." Ben hastily formulated a plan to get Aston's car back. "You really thought you would get away with it?"

The petrified expression the kid wore convinced Ben this crew had never even considered they might fail. He didn't know whether to find that sort of bravery and confidence impressive or utterly stupid.

Ben rose to his full height and pointed at the youngest kid in the crew. He had finally come around after Devil dropped him with that punch. The little bastard probably wasn't even out of high school yet. "You're going to take my men to the junk yard to get our cars."

"Y-yes, sir."

Ben gave orders for half of his crew to head for the junk yard. One of his men asked if he should kill the kid and leave him in the trunk of a car, but Ben shook his head.

The rest of the men were left with Devil to guard their prisoners and the club. When he stepped away from the group, his scarred friend followed him. Before Ben asked, Devil presented him with the keys to his truck. "Try not to wreck this one, huh?"

"I'll do my best." He glanced around the club and then at the group of young men huddled together in the center of the dance floor. They were starting to separate into small cliques, wiggling away from each other and betraying their mistrust. It was a sad sight. There was no unity in this crew and nothing to bind them together. They would fracture after tonight and this upstart gang would be reduced to a cautionary tale. *This is what happens when you raid an eagle's nest.*

Addressing him in Albanian so their captives wouldn't understand, Devil asked, "What do you want me to do with them?"

"They're thieves." It was all he had to say.

"And the club?"

"Burn it."

As he left the building gripping his bound prisoner by the back of the neck, Ben experienced the briefest pang of guilt and regret at how easily he gave such terrible orders. He shoved the kid into the passenger seat and buckled his seat belt. Not because he wanted to keep him safe but to deter him from trying to bail while they drove.

The rap music grew louder as Ben backed out of the parking spot. No doubt Devil had turned up the volume to hide the wailing cries that would soon erupt when he unsheathed that wicked knife of his. His passenger noticed and swallowed loudly. "Are you going to kill my friends?"

"Not tonight," he answered honestly. "Do you know what we do to thieves?"

The kid shook his head so Ben lifted his hand and wiggled his pointer finger. His captive paled and looked sick. "It's a small price," Ben reminded him. "It's a hell of a lot better than a knife to the throat."

"Yeah," he weakly agreed. "It wasn't personal, you know? We didn't want to cross you or Lalo, but Calvin is our boss-"

Ben couldn't help himself. He laughed at the absurdity of it. "He's your *boss?* What? You guys think you're starting up your own little mafia?" When the kid didn't answer, he realized that's exactly what they thought they were doing. "Are you really that fucking stupid? Do you know who runs this town?"

"Nikolai Kalasnikov."

"Did you think he was going to let some new outfit shoulder their way into the inner circle and upset the careful balance he maintains? Huh?"

"Calvin said that with Besian out of town and the cartel about to start a civil war, we could take what we wanted. He said this was the time to strike. He said-"

"I don't give a shit what Calvin said. I asked what *you* thought would happen if you made this move."

"I didn't think. I just...I wanted it. I wanted it *all."*

"That greed is going to get you killed."

"Tonight?"

Ben didn't answer because he honestly wasn't sure. Lalo would want the kid's head as a deterrent for anyone else who thought they could steal from one of his dealers. Though it wasn't a pleasant thought, Ben recognized that it would be easier to get Baby back from Lalo if he gave him the kid as a gift. Could he do that?

His lack of a reply silenced the kid who gripped the seatbelt with shaking hands. The sight of all that trembling made him remember the first night he had been thrown into the adult side of the jail. One of his mother's rich and well-connected customers had managed to get him out the next morning but that night he had been terrified. He hadn't grown into his full height or bulked up yet so he was smaller and easily subdued, especially with the group of men jammed into that cell.

But Devil had been there that night. He had never met the man everyone in the Albanian crew called *Dreq,* but one look at that face and he had known. Somehow Devil had recognized him as Seline's son and Besian's sort-of ward. He had kept Ben safe that night. Two days later, Devil started training him to fight and build muscle. Within six months, he had been the mafia's newest enforcer. The rest was history.

"Left at the next light," the kid said finally. "You know Carston's Floors and More?" When Ben nodded, he said, "It's closed now and the building is empty. It's a good hiding place."

Within five minutes, they were parked in the alley behind the bankrupt business. The kid squeezed in through a broken window and Ben had no choice but to follow him. He did it carefully and with his weapon at the ready. If this little shit tried to attack him, he wouldn't hesitate. He wasn't going to let anyone rob him of the chance to slide back into bed with Aston.

The kid grabbed a couple of flashlights from a work table and handed one over to him. Ben flicked it on and used it to do a quick sweep of the place. Most of the inventory had been cleared out during the final blowout sale, but there were still pallets of tile, rolls of carpet and boxes of laminate flooring stacked around the storeroom. With a wave of his flashlight beam, he gestured for the kid to keep moving.

In the far corner of the storeroom, hidden behind rolls of thick, blue carpet, sat two pallets loaded down with more drugs than Ben had ever seen at one time. It was an absolute fucking fortune in product and the biggest take their family had ever gotten over on another crew. He prayed the extra cash would soften Besian's anger when the time came.

Digging out his phone, Ben called Zee and hoped the infamous international smuggler had landed in Houston. When the call went to voicemail, his hope deflated. Before he had tucked it back into his pocket, the phone began to ring and his hope flared to life again. "Zee?"

"I hear we have a little problem." The gravelly voice that greeted him inspired a chill deep in his chest. Though Zee had never treated him with anything but respect, he had heard about the man's peculiar appetites. There weren't many people who scared Ben but Zee was one of them.

"I took care of it. We'll have the cars in hand soon." He eyed the baggies and bricks in front of him. "I have something you'll want to see."

"Is that so?"

"Yes." He rattled off the address of the building. "I'll be here."

"Alone?"

Ben glanced at the kid who held the flashlight between his bound hands and swallowed anxiously. Glad they were speaking Albanian, he said, "Yes."

The phone call ended, and Ben tucked away the phone. He stared at the kid for a moment. "What's your name?"

"Tayshaun."

"How old are you?"

"Nineteen."

Ben's jaw clenched. "Do you have family?"

"I've got a sister up in Dallas."

"That's it?"

"She's got three kids."

"And a husband?"

"No."

"Boyfriend?"

"No. She's alone. She works nights as a nurse in one of the emergency rooms there."

Ben's gaze slid to the shelves behind Tayshaun. He crossed to them, quietly and with purpose, and grasped the handle of the tile knife there. Tayshaun's breath hitched. For a moment, Ben thought he might try to run, but the kid finally found the courage to man up and face what was coming to him.

"Can you make sure my sister-?"

"You can tell her whatever it is you want to say when you see her later." Ben snatched Tayshaun's hands and cut the rope binding them together. He dragged one hand to the nearest table and steeled himself for the blood that would soon cover its surface.

"You're letting me go?"

"I'm giving you a chance I never had." He pressed the edge of the knife into the kid's throat, nicking his darker skin and watching the blood pool along the silver edge of the blade. "If you're smart, you'll get out of town immediately. You don't call anyone. You don't text anyone. You forget about everyone you ever knew in Houston. You run to Dallas, and you never look back." He pushed the blade a little harder against Tayshaun's throat. "If I ever find out you came back here--"

"I won't," he swore it like a vow. "I'll leave right now."

"You had better. Lalo Contreras will have your dick for what you've done. Do you understand?"

"Yes."

Ben tried not to think about where this sudden burst of mercy had originated. Less than a night in Aston McNeil's company and already he was getting soft. Besian would smack the shit out of him if he could see him now. Disgusted with his own weakness, he moved the knife to Tayshaun's finger.

Flattening his hand on the tabletop, the kid inhaled a shaky breath. "Do it, man. Just do it!"

So he did.

5 CHAPTER FIVE

My ringing cell phone dragged me out of a fitful sleep. Inhaling sharply, I scrubbed a hand down my face and reached for my phone. Without looking at the screen, I swiped my finger across it and lifted the device to my ear. "Hello?"

"Aston."

My stepbrother's deceptively warm voice jerked me fully awake. "Calvin. Where are you?"

"Well, it's an interesting thing. You see, I have Baby. In fact, I'm sitting in her right now. With a can of gasoline and a box of matches, " he added with a shrill laugh. "Can you imagine the bonfire? It's going to be beautiful, probably even prettier than the time I burned all of your mother's photos."

My stomach churned painfully at the memory. He had gathered up every photo of her in the house along with her wedding dress and other mementos my father had kept for me, taken them outside and thrown them into a flaming fire pit. That had been the night Daddy finally realized I wasn't being a jealous, petty little girl who wanted to break up his new marriage. It was also the last night Calvin had lived in our home. By the next morning, he had been packed off to a military academy. Not that it had helped any...

Tired of his cruel games, I sighed with resignation. "What do you want?"

"I want what's mine."

"And what is that? You were given everything that was promised to you in the will." I had given him more than that, actually, in the hopes that he would go away and never bother me again.

"I want my father's company." His venomous voice made me shudder. "Jack stole it from me the same way he stole my mother."

He sounded like a petulant child. It occurred to me that he might be a man in age, but he was perpetually frozen as a bitter, sadistic little boy. "Is that what this is about? Is this why you've been tormenting me since we were kids?"

"I tormented you because it made me laugh to see you cry. If you weren't so fucking weak, I might have stopped after the night I gave you to Russ, after your father finally understood what it felt like to have someone take something precious from you."

The way he spoke made me wonder what Russ had told him about that night. Had Russ lied about raping me to protect me from Calvin? Had my father gone along with the lie and allowed Calvin to think he had succeeded in his vicious trick to protect me? As far as I knew, Russ and Calvin had never spoken again after that night. Was there another man I owed a favor and a debt of gratitude?

"The company is gone, Calvin. It was completely dissolved."

"Not all of it," he argued. "Jack kept everything from the research and development department of Darbin Industries inside his safe."

I tried to remember exactly what the company my father had gobbled up in one of his acquisitions actually did. It was something to do with satellites. After Calvin's father had been arrested for drunk driving, the company's revenues had tanked. A few months later, he had died in a small-engine plane crash. Shortly after Daddy acquired Darbin Industries, he had started dating Marjorie. Calvin had been fourteen then. Had it looked as if my father was taking everything away from him? Even so, that was no excuse to do the awful things he had done.

"Is that why you ransacked the house while we were burying Daddy?"

"Your stupidity never ceases to amaze me. Of course! Do you really think I gave two squirts of piss about cuff links and jewelry? Now, listen to me, Aston. I'm waiting at the house. You have exactly sixty minutes to get here and unlock that safe or else I'll burn this whole fucking house down with Baby in it."

He wasn't bluffing. He would do it. Hell, he was probably going to do it even if I gave him everything out of the safe.

"I'll be there."

"One hour, Aston-and come alone. Don't even think about bringing that Neanderthal mobster you've been fucking all night."

The revelation that he had been following me hit me like a wave of cold water. Suddenly nervous, I dropped the phone, slid out of bed and reached for my clothes. Was he watching me now? Had he hired someone to keep tabs on me? Knowing that he had Baby, I had to accept that he had instructed those men in the SUVs to try to kill us.

He's insane. You can't go meet him. He'll kill you.

But I was so tired of being afraid of him.

My gaze landed on the matte black pistol Ben had left behind. Picking it up, I tested the weight of it and squeezed the grip. As a backup piece, it was smaller and lighter than the type of weapon a man like Ben would normally carry, but it was perfect for me.

As I got dressed, I remembered what I had promised him. I picked up my phone to call him and let him know that I was leaving, but he hadn't given me his number. I didn't know how to reach him. I doubted anyone was at the auto shop this early. Would anyone even answer if I called?

I couldn't meet Calvin without telling someone so I sent a text message to the only person in the world I trusted without reservation. If anyone could help me now, it was Marley.

"Well?" Ben watched Zee poke through the massive stash of drugs.

"**I** can move this easy. I won't pay full price, not even to you and Besian, because **I'm** going to have to be careful about sending this far away to avoid a clash with the Guzman cartel. You'll still get a nice cut."

"I'm not worried about my cut. The money will go to my crew. After tonight's problems, they deserve it." He glanced at the four guards who traveled with Zee. "Can you handle this?"

Zee rose from his crouched position. The shadows hid his face but the glow of a flashlight illuminated the open collar of his shirt. The gnarly scar he bore from a razor that had slashed open his throat was hidden beneath a tattoo that served as a reminder of what he had survived. It also reminded Ben that he had just asked the stupidest question ever.

"Are you that hot to get back to that sweet little heiress you've got tucked away at Alina's?"

Annoyed that he could never have even one secret, he growled, "Did they put us in one of the rooms with the peepholes?"

"No, but when a young woman like Aston McNeil walks into a brothel with one of our men, Alina knows that it's something I want to know." He let loose a laugh. "I would have loved to have seen that girl's face when she realized you had led her right into the most exclusive brothel in Texas."

"It was the only place I could take her."

"I agree." His mouth curved with a teasing grin. "And did you *take* her?"

" Jesus, you and Devil are worse than a bunch of gossiping old women, you know that? What I do with my dick is my business."

"Until it becomes mine or Besian's," he warned carefully. "Have fun with her if you like. Fuck her for the rest of the weekend if she's good-and then get rid of her." Zee squeezed his shoulder with a brutal hand that Ben knew had done some truly terrible things. "She's beautiful, and I don't blame you for wanting something so precious, but you can't have her. She's too high profile, and she'll bring too much attention to the family."

Ben wanted to argue, but he clenched his teeth together and nodded. Zec's hand moved to the back of his head in an almost fatherly gesture. They shared a silent look. For the first time, Ben saw beyond the soulless blackness of Zec's gaze. For the briefest of seconds, he caught a glimpse of something vulnerable and sad.

But then it was gone, the moment so fleeting Ben questioned whether it had happened at all.

Zee pulled back his hand and cleared his throat. "If you're starting to feel like you want something real and not just a tumble with one of the dancing girls, tell me and I'll find a good girl for you. One of us," he said pointedly. "Someone of our blood. Someone we can trust."

The thought of letting a man like Zee act as his matchmaker was too much for Ben to even consider. He put up his hands. "I'm going. Call Devil. He'll have the cars by now."

Zee pushed the two severed fingers across the table with the tip of the blade Ben had used to separate them from Tayshaun's hand. One would be given to their boss as the payment for the honor debt he owed for stealing those cars. The other would go to Lalo. "Where are you going?"

"To get the Aston Martin," he said matter-of-factly.

"For my delivery?" Zee called after him.

Ben didn't dare ignore him, but the smuggler wasn't going to like the answer. "No."

He half-expected Zec's guards to accost him and drag him back, but they let him pass. Out in Devil's truck, he fired up the ignition and backed out of the alley. He hadn't been to Lalo's house in a few weeks, not since he had delivered that last modified car for the dealer, so he decided to call ahead, especially since it was so damned early in the morning. The call went to voicemail so he left a short message.

No sooner had he ended the call than his phone started ringing. He glanced at the number but didn't recognize it. With a thud, he remembered that he hadn't exchanged contact information with Aston. Even if she wanted to reach him, she couldn't. Unless she had gotten brave enough to venture outside the room where he had left her to find Alina and ask.

"Aston?"

"You gave her a gun!"

Taken aback by the furious voice on the other end of the phone, it took him a moment to place it. "Marley? How did you get this number?"

"How do you think I got it? I asked Spider." She huffed and panted and sounded as if she were trying to get dressed as quickly as possible. "What the hell were you thinking giving Aston a gun?"

"I was trying to protect her." His stomach knotted with dread. "Marley, where is Aston? Why are you calling me?"

"She sent me a text about twenty minutes ago. I didn't see it until I got up to get a drink. She's gone to meet Calvin. He has Baby."

"No, he doesn't." Panic gripped his heart like a vise. "Where is she meeting him?"

"At her house," Marley said, the rattle of keys filling his ear. "I'm heading there now."

"Give me the address." He pulled over long enough to punch in her house number and street for the GPS unit. "I'm fifteen minutes from her house. Where are you?"

"Too far," Marley said, her voice tight. "I'll hurry, but you better get there first. You don't know what he's like. You don't know what he's capable of doing."

"I'll get there." He hung up and dropped the phone onto the seat before checking the rearview mirror and merging back into traffic. If Aston had sent her message twenty minutes ago and she had left the brothel around that time, she wouldn't reach her home in Royal Oaks for another ten minutes or so. That would only put him a few minutes behind her.

Stupid, stupid, stupid, he silently berated himself. How could he have been so foolish? He had left behind the gun not because he intended her to actually use the damned thing but because he had hoped it would make her feel more at ease knowing she had a way to defend herself. He had hoped she would be able to rest and stay safe while he sorted out this clusterfuck.

Now she was running off to confront her psycho stepbrother with the gun he had stupidly thrust into her hands. If she got hurt, he would never forgive himself. Hell, if she got hurt, he would probably end up on the pointy end of a knife Marley borrowed from Spider. That friend of Aston's had a sweet, soft gentleness about her, but he had heard the tales of her biological father. If she had inherited even a drop of his bad blood, she would flay him alive for exposing her best friend to harm. He would deserve it.

The moment they had escaped the 1-8-7 crew trying to gun them down, he should have driven her straight to a police station. He should have urged her to file a police report on the stolen car and to say that he had kidnapped her and nearly gotten her shot. They would have taken her into protective custody and kept her guarded around the clock.

But he hadn't done that. He'd dragged her to a brothel, seduced her and then left her with a gun and a promise of his return. Shame roiled in his gut and left him feeling sick with himself. Zee was wrong. He didn't need to stay away from Aston because she was too high profile. He needed to stay away from her because she deserved a better man.

A better class of man. Wasn't that what she had said after she smacked him in his office? She had been right. He was too low class and mobbed up to ever be trusted with a woman like her.

Mercifully, there were no gates guarding the entrance to her neighborhood. Just as he had expected, the mansions here were oversized and sumptuous with their pretentious architecture and manicured lawns. It was yet another reminder that this world of Aston's would never be his anymore than his could ever be hers.

He found her house number and turned down the private drive that angled away from the street. Huge pecan and oak trees provided a thick barrier that shrouded the house. He spotted the Camara parked in front but didn't see another vehicle. Ben refused to believe her stepbrother had gotten his hands on the Aston Martin. It was nothing more than a ruse to lure her close.

But Calvin had gotten more than he had bargained for with his lure. Ben had given Aston his word. Calvin would never hurt her again.

Even if that meant he had to put her stepbrother six feet underground.

CHAPTER SIX

I realized my mistake the second I stepped into the house. The cold, hard tip of a knife pressed into the soft skin of my throat. I gulped and closed my eyes. *So this is how it ends.*

"Close the door. Give me your phone."

I did exactly as Calvin ordered and made sure to keep my movements slow and small lest he cut me open with the knife he held to my neck. He didn't frisk me for a weapon. If he had run his hand along my back, he would have felt the rigid outline of the gun hidden there. The layers of my top and jacket concealed it for now.

"Don't think about screaming for Nina and Pedro. They're not here."

My chest constricted with fear for the married housekeeper and groundskeeper who had lived in this house and worked for my family since before I was born. "Did you kill them?"

His laughter made my skin scrawl. "No. I paid a cop to call with a fake report of their son's mJury. They're probably hitting San Antonio right about now. So it's just you and me now, sis."

"Lucky me," I said, finally daring to look into his eyes.

He let the point of the knife glide down the exposed skin of my throat until it was nestled between my breasts and pressing against my heart. The long line he had scratched into my skin burned and throbbed. "This might be your luckiest night yet." He dragged the knife along the swell of my breast. "Russ said you didn't scream when he took you that night in the pool house, but I've always wondered if it was the drugs or because you actually liked it. "

I glared at him. "Fuck. You."

"Later, sweetness," he said with that evil smile I had come to loathe. "I've always wanted to throw you face down across your beloved Daddy's desk. God, I hope he haunts this place. I'm getting hard just thinking about his ghost watching us."

I swallowed hard as bile rose in my throat. "You are such a sick freak."

"Blah, blah, blah," he intoned in a high-pitched voice while talking with his hand. "Like I haven't heard that from fifty psychologists." He pressed the knife back to the curve of my throat. "Walk. Now."

"Where?"

"The office, obviously," he added tersely. "We're going to open up that big ole safe Jack had hidden behind the bookcase there."

A quiver of panic pierced my belly. "I don't know the combination."

"Don't even try that bullshit with me." He purposely nicked my neck to remind me of my precarious position. "He gave you everything before he died. I know he gave you the combination."

"Not to that safe," I hurriedly replied. "Really. I've tried to open it a million times."

"Well, for your sake, I hope one million and one is your lucky number." The knife dug into my throat even harder. "Walk."

When we made it to my father's office, the one room in the house I hadn't dared touch since his death, he shoved me toward the bookcase. I stumbled into it and narrowly missed hitting my cheek. Righting myself, I found the button hidden along the underside of the panel and pressed it. The bookcase popped away from the wall and swung to the side on hidden hinges to reveal the safe.

"Open it." He pushed me to my knees in front of the keypad.

Lifting shaky fingers to the buttons, I tried to remember all the combinations I had tried since my father's death. My birthday, his birthday, my Social Security number, his, my mother's birthday, the day my mother died, the date of his first marriage, the date of the second to Marjorie-none of them worked. As I considered what Calvin thought this safe contained, it finally hit me. "What was the date of the acquisition?"

"What? Of course!" He grasped my shoulders and flung me out of the way. "Move!"

Before I could react, he had opened the safe and started dragging out armfuls of envelopes and cardboard tubes. He pried the cap off one tube, upended it-and nothing but ashes poured onto the rug. I watched with a mixture of dread and fascination as tube after tube and envelope after envelope yielded nothing but ashes, burnt scraps of paper, crushed flash drives and shredded discs.

Calvin grew more agitated and angry. He cursed a blue streak while dumping out the contents of each package. I couldn't help it. I started laughing. Hysterically.

"What the fuck is the matter with you?" Calvin demanded as he whirled on me. "You think this is funny?" He slapped a handful of ash in my face. "Is this hilarious to you?"

Wiping ash from my face and certain I must have looked crazy, I nodded. "I think it's the funniest thing I've ever seen in my life. Daddy destroyed the one thing you wanted. Even from the grave, he found a way to give you the biggest middle finger imaginable."

"Yeah? You want to talk about graves? Let's talk about my mother's. Do you really think it was an accident that those cupcakes had ground up macadamia nuts in them and that her Epi-Pen malfunctioned?"

My laughter died, and the smile faded from my face. "What are you saying?"

"I'm saying that I killed that traitorous bitch. She married the man who ruined my father's company-"

"Your father ruined his own company."

"Your father was lucky you had so many nurses watching him and that you slept in his room around the clock there at the end," Calvin sneered. "I had the perfect end planned for him." His manic smile returned. "But no matter. Now it's time for my real masterpiece."

He wielded his knife like an expert and flew at me. I scuttled out of the way and slung the closest chair in between us. He tripped over it and hit his face on the floor. When I threw the chair at him, the movement freed the gun tucked into the waistband of my skirt. It hit the floor with a loud *thunk.*

Calvin snarled and dove for the gun, but I got there first. Before I could flick off the safety, he slapped it out of my hands. We scrambled across the floor toward the weapon, our elbows jamming together and our hands smacking. He snatched up the pistol and swung it toward me, but I locked my hands together and used the momentum of both arms to hit him in the face. He managed to get a good smack in, but I put both hands against his chin and shoved hard. He tried to bring the gun toward me and almost succeeded-until a big leather boot connected with his head.

My tattooed knight in leather and denim appeared suddenly and miraculously. The kick he landed to Calvin's head dazed my stepbrother long enough for Ben to take him down to the floor. I clambered out of the way, crawling backwards toward the door and unable to look away as Ben used those powerful arms and strong hands of his to throttle Calvin.

Somehow my stepbrother had managed to keep a grip on the pistol. He pointed it toward Ben's head, but Ben blocked it at the last moment. The crack of the gunshot ricocheted off the coffered ceilings and marble floors. I screamed, but Ben proved his prowess in a fight by ripping the gun away from Calvin and pistol-whipping him into submission.

"Aston!"

Shocked by Marley's voice, I glanced at the doorway just in time to see her rush through it. Her eyes widened at the bloody sight before her, but my eyes widened at the sight of Devil running toward her back. He grabbed her by the shoulders and set her aside like one might an unruly child. His long legs ate up the floor as he came to Ben's aid.

When Ben jerked a knife from a scabbard hidden in his boot, I reacted on instinct. "No! Ben! Don't!"

His wild-eyed gaze landed on me. He held the knife to Calvin's neck, ready to slit him wide open. My stepbrother gurgled and coughed as he fought to breathe. The gurgles soon turned to laughter. He was laughing like a hyena, barking with sheer delight and making all of us look at him in horror.

Panting, Ben stated the obvious. "He tried to kill you. He tried to have you raped by his friend. He stole from you. He tried to shoot us both tonight. He damned near kicked off a war with a cartel."

"I know," I said quietly, accepting everything he said as truth. "He killed his mother too. He planned to rape me before he was done tonight."

Ben's expression slackened and then grew fierce like a warrior. "He'll only try to hurt you again. He'll keep hurting other people." Ben brought the knife tight against Calvin's jugular. "He needs to die."

"I know-but it can't be you."

Our gazes held for a tense moment. Ben's jaw worked back and forth. Did he understand why it couldn't be him? Did he understand that I couldn't bear the thought of Calvin's blood staining his hands forever?

Sitting back on his heels, Ben lowered the knife and glanced at Marley. "Take Aston to her room. Get her cleaned up."

Marley nodded shakily and grasped my upper arm. "Come on, Aston. Let's go."

Clinging to my best friend, I stumbled out of the office. I didn't dare look back as she led me upstairs. We could hear the low murmuring of male voices-and then there was only silence. We both knew what that meant, but neither of us spoke aloud what we were thinking.

She closed my bedroom door, turned on the light and tugged me into the bathroom. I caught a glimpse of my face in the mirror. I had a swollen cheek with a small cut under my eye. The nick on my neck had bled more than I had imagined, and the gnarly scratch was bright red and angry.

"You'll feel better once you're clean." She pushed me toward the shower. "I'm going downstairs to get you something to drink."

"Water," I said, my voice husky.

"And something stronger," she added knowingly. "Food, too. You're bound to get the shakes soon."

As she left and I undressed, I found myself wondering if she had gone through all this after being kidnapped and narrowly escaped an assassin's bullet. Safe inside the shower, I let the hot water rush over my tired body. Every time I closed my eyes, I saw Calvin's crazed face. I could hear him telling me how he had killed his mother and how he wanted to hurt and kill me. His manic laughter echoed in my ears.

Footsteps in the bathroom alerted me to Marley's return. With my back to the entrance of the walk-in shower, I asked, "Do you want to stay for the rest of the night?"

"Yes."

I spun around at the low, raspy answer. It wasn't Marley eyeing me like a predator but Ben. He had stripped down to only his jeans and those were quickly whisked away along with his boxers and socks. Joining me in the shower, he cupped my face and lowered his mouth until it brushed mine. He kissed me tenderly and so sweetly that I had to blink away tears. His thumbs gently caressed my cheeks. "Are you all right?"

Figuring he was one of the few people who might understand what I was feeling, I admitted, "I'm relieved, but that's wrong, isn't it?"

He shook his head. "Calvin is rotten. He's psychotic. He's *dangerous."*

"Is?" I seized on the word. "You didn't...?"

"Not yet," Ben said, reaching for one of the sponges resting in the corner basket. "I refused to dishonor your home in that way. Devil took him."

"Where?"

"I don't know." He lathered up the sponge with my favorite body wash. "You'll never see him again."

"The police?"

"You don't need to worry about that."

Licking my lips, I asked, "Where is Marley?"

"She left a tray in your bedroom. She said she's staying across the hall. Apparently you refused to leave her after she was kidnapped. Now she's refusing to leave you." He pressed a gentle kiss to my forehead. "You're lucky to have a friend like that."

"I know."

"You're a strange pair, the two of you." He dragged the foamy sponge up my arm, across my back and down the other arm. "You'll have to tell me how a girl from a trailer park and a girl from Royal Oaks managed to become such good friends."

"Tomorrow," I said, enjoying the feel of the soapy sponge gliding over my skin too much.

"All right." He swiped long lines along my back and slow circles on my belly. Eventually, he abandoned the sponge in favor of his hands. I leaned back against the tiles and closed my eyes, relishing the feel of his rough, warm palms moving over my skin. His mouth found mine, and I reacted with the usual heat and need that his touch inspired.

Breaking away, he growled. "I want you."

"So have me."

"No, you just survived-"

"Yes," I interrupted, clasping his face. "I survived. I'm *alive*. Now help me enjoy it."

That was all the permission he needed. Shutting off the water, he swung me up in his arms and carefully left the bathroom. With anyone else, I would have complained about the watery trail we were leaving, but with Ben I just didn't care. I wanted him. *Now.*

He put me on the bed so very gently. There was no mistaking the passion blazing in his pale green eyes, but he touched me so softly and with such caution. Certain he was afraid of scaring me, I pushed up on my elbows and captured his mouth with an insistent kiss. A rumbling groan erupted from his throat, and I smiled knowingly.

Interlacing our fingers, Ben trailed ticklish kisses down the side of my face and along my neck. He spent extra time kissing the wounds Calvin had left behind, his sensual touch erasing the bad memories. Down and down he went, his lips pressing here and there and making me sigh with pleasure. He suckled my nipples and grazed his teeth over them, causing me to buck up against his bigger, stronger body.

Chuckling with amusement at my reaction, Ben sought out new ways to make me mewl like a kitten and arch my back. **His** tongue dragged a zigzag line to my navel and then back to my chest. His hand caressed my belly and hips before sliding between my thighs.

He brushed his knuckles down the seam of my pussy while tormenting my breasts with his mouth. His thick fingers parted my folds. He slid one down to my entrance and found me already wet, but he didn't penetrate me yet. His fingertips danced around my clitoris, swirling over the swollen nub and making me pant. Tangling his fingers in my wet hair, he forced me to hold his heated gaze while he carefully thrust one long digit into my slick sheath. He was testing me, ensuring I was ready for him when the time came. A second finger joined the first. His thumb flicked my clit while his curved fingers glided in and out of me. I clenched around his thrusting digits and wished they were his cock.

He must have been able to read my mind because he carefully pulled his hand away from me. I nearly died when he licked my shiny nectar from his fingers. He grinned at my embarrassment and made my face even hotter when he nuzzled my ear and whispered, "You have the sweetest, juiciest cunt. I could eat you all night and still want more."

Head pounding and dizzy, I clutched at his shoulders when he moved between my thighs. My legs fell open for him in silent invitation. His wolfish, sinful grin made my heart flip-flop in my chest. I moaned with anticipation as he kissed my knees and thighs and dipped his tongue into my navel before sliding between my parted thighs. The fat head of his cock rubbed against my leg and then my lower belly. I trembled as need flared in my core and seared me with its heat.

Wanting to touch him, I grasped his rigid length and marveled yet again at the size of him. He shivered as my hand pumped him from blunt crown to wide base. I let my hand slide even lower to cup his heavy sac. His nostrils flared, and he sent me a promising look. Now it was my turn to grin wickedly. I had no doubt that making love to Ben would eclipse every other experience.

Holding his cock, I guided him into place. His hand settled on thc back of my neck just before he breached me. With one long, deliberate thrust, he impaled me. His pale eyes never left mine. I gasped at the sudden invasion, my body unused to anything so big or thick. The concerned expression he wore told me Ben understood. I didn't need to worry. He wasn't going to hurt me.

Fully sheathed in my pussy, he claimed my mouth with languid, lazy kisses. His hips started to move, and he took me with slow, easy strokes. Those skilled hands of his rode my curves, palming my breasts and pinching my nipples before settling on my waist. I couldn't stop touching him either. My greedy hands moved over his tattoos. I wanted to know all the stories behind the symbols he had chosen to forever mark his body. One night with Ben was never going to be enough.

The frantic way he plundered my mouth and his tightening grip on my waist convinced me he felt the same way. I cried out when he bit the fleshy curve of my neck, his teeth sinking in enough to leave a bruise. When he sucked hard on the spot, laving it with his tongue, my pussy clenched around his thrusting cock. I clawed at his back, scratching at him and pulling him in closer.

Laughing at my wanton behavior, Ben sneaked his hand between our bodies, landing right above the spot where we were joined together. He nibbled my lower lip, and I remembered the way he had teased and nibbled other parts of me. His fingertips danced around my clit the same way his tongue had earlier that night. I gazed into his green eyes, his irises smoky with lust, and felt a quiver of panic. What if this was it? What if this moment was the last one we would share together?

Ben's fingers swirled in the wetness coating that pink pearl hidden away between my thighs. My worries were forgotten as his tongue stabbed against mine. Clutching his shoulders, I surrendered to that shuddery, blissful throb building in my lower belly. I whispered his name on a sigh and he smiled at me. "That's it, baby. Come with me."

I shattered beneath him, hips rocking and back arching. I tossed back my head as I cried out with pleasure and squeezed my thighs around his waist. Ben tasted my mouth again, drowning out my screams, and started to pound into me. He was wild with me now. His hips snapped at a breakneck pace, and his cock pounded me into the mattress. All I could do was hold on and ride the incredible and seemingly unending waves of ecstasy.

When he grasped my calves and lifted my ankles to his shoulders, I moaned noisily. His eyes had taken on a predatory shine, and I knew then that I was really going to get it now. He gripped my ankles hard enough to leave bruises and fucked me like no one ever had-or ever would. It was always going to be Ben that I remembered when I closed my eyes and conjured up my most wanted fantasy. It was always going to be this rough, impossibly sexy mob enforcer who had saved my life by stealing my car.

"Ben! Oh! *Please."*

He let my legs fall to his waist again. With his one hand planted near my head, he threaded his fingers through my hair and claimed my mouth. The passion and power of his kiss left me reeling. His forehead touched mine, our noses bumping together as we panted and shared each other's air, and then he slammed so hard and deep that I slid up the bed. He jerked against me-and then I felt it.

At the same moment, we locked gazes. In the frantic heat of our coupling, we had forgotten the most important thing of all. As shudders wracked his body, he spilled his blazing hot seed inside me. I had no idea it would feel so different without that latex barrier. My heart raced but not with fear. I didn't dare put a name to the primal sensation.

Ben's eyes closed as a shiver coursed through him. When he looked at me again, I easily read the shame, guilt and pleasure on his face. He started to say something but I stopped him by placing my fingers to his mouth. I refused to let him ruin this perfectly perfect moment. Ben seemed to understand what I couldn't say and nodded before kissing each of my fingertips.

When he finally pulled away from me and tucked me against his chest, I went willingly and with a smile. Exhaustion took us both. Curled together we slept until the first grayish pink rays of sunshine were streaming into my bedroom. I came awake to the sensation of Ben's soft lips peppering kisses across my back and along my neck. When I wiggled my hips, I felt his cock nudging my bottom. Half-asleep but already burning with desire, I pushed back against him.

"We shouldn't, Aston." His voice was gravelly with sleep.

I pressed against his erection, but he didn't move toward me. Annoyed, I reached back to fondle him. "We really should."

Not one to be dominated, Ben grasped my waist and shifted me into the position he wanted. I smiled at the way he used that brute strength of his to lift me up in the bed and shove my thighs open. Spooning me, he thrust inside a few inches, pulled back and slid in deeper. I whimpered with need and reached back to grip his hip. My hand traveled lower and settled on his taut ass. I loved the way his muscles rippled beneath my palm.

Wanting it hard and rough like the first time, I tried to get what I desired by pressing down to meet his thrusts. "Ben, I want-"

"No." His lips brushed my ear. "Not this time."

"But-"

"No." As if to show me who was boss, he slid his arm under my body and clamped it across my breasts. He held me against his chest and took me slow and easy. Instead of the wildfire that had burned through me earlier, this was steady and grew hotter with each passing minute. I closed my eyes and held onto his arm, letting him take me and trusting him to give me what I needed.

Ben dragged my hand to his mouth and sucked on my fingers. He flicked his tongue over them, wetting my skin, and then pushed my hand down to the juncture of my thighs. "Touch yourself," he ordered gruffly. "Make yourself come for me."

He must have known that he was one of the few people in the world who could get away with telling me to do anything. Not that I was going to put up much fight about an instruction like that one. Finding that swollen bundle of nerves, I strummed it the way I liked most. Ben's thrusts were faster now but still too achingly slow. He nuzzled my neck and whispered in my ear, telling me how beautiful and brave I was. He teethed my earlobe before changing the angle of his hips. The new way his cock stroked inside me was too good. I curled my toes against his shin and whimpered.

"That's it," he murmured. "Let go, baby. Let go for me."

The moment his strong hand encircled my throat, a frisson of panic raced through my belly. He wasn't going to do *that* but it was the possibility of danger, however slim, that set me off. He lovingly cupped my neck in that big hand of his while I cried out with pleasure, calling his name and clutching at his forearm. The wicked spasms of my pussy gripped his thrusting cock, enhancing the fluttery bursts of joy that exploded in my belly.

"Aston!" He growled my name as he climaxed. "Aston. *Aston."*

Stay. I bit my tongue rather than say that one word. It was a silly thought. A stupid one, actually. There was no way Ben reciprocated my feelings. Enthralled by the glimmer of possibility, I desperately wanted to roll over, kiss him and ask him to stay, to give whatever this was that had sparked off between us, a real try.

Losing myself in the warmth of Ben's protective arms, I stayed awake a little longer after he had fallen back asleep. An unwanted feeling crept from the pit of my stomach and into my chest. I knew what was coming. I knew what would happen once I fell asleep, but I fought a losing battle and soon succumbed to my exhaustion again.

And when I woke, I found my bed empty. The sheets were cold on the side where he had slept. A single sheet of paper taken from my small desk across the room rested on the pillow. I picked it up and scanned the short message he had scrawled for me.

I'll call you.

But he didn't.

7 CHAPTER SEVEN

"Ben?"

Surprised by Besian's voice, he lowered his socket wrench and stepped out from under the car lift. The boss rarely made an appearance at the shop. **In** his dark suit and shiny shoes, he looked totally out of place amid the dust and the grime, but Ben knew better than to think the expensive clothes had made the man soft. He might be a successful and mostly legitimate businessman now, but he had clawed his way to power with vicious and brutal acts that he wouldn't hesitate to repeat again.

"Boss." He tugged a rag from the back pocket of his jeans and cleaned his dirty fingers. "I didn't know you were coming by today."

Besian gestured toward the open garage doors and the stillness of the evening. "Meet me outside." His gaze slid to Ben's filthy clothes. "Change your jeans, at least. You don't want to stain these seats."

He stuffed the rag into his pocket. "Give me five minutes."

After ducking into his office to grab the extra pair of clothes he kept on hand, he slipped into the employee bathroom to scrub away the grease and grime coating his hands. He stared at his reflection as he dried his hands and wiped a soapy paper towel over his face and along the back of his neck. There were lines under his eyes and around his mouth. He hadn't been sleeping well, not since...

Not since you left Aston like a fucking coward.

His stomach churned with the memory of leaving sweet, beguiling Aston and sneaking out of her house. He had taken the stolen Camara to Zec's new holding spot. The smuggler had taken one look at him and then patted his back in a comforting way. He had wanted to be angry at Zee for forcing him to acknowledge the ugly truth of the situation, but he couldn't muster the energy for it. Instead, he had wel-corned the cold numbness that had spread through him.

Crumpling up the soggy towel, he tossed it in the trash and made quick work of changing his clothes. He caught Devil's eye after he locked up his office. The scarred giant waved to let him know he had the shop under control.

Out in the still, muggy night, he heard a car idling down the street. He walked toward the sound but stopped abruptly when the silver Aston Martin came into view. Although he had tried to get the namesake car back, Besian had forbidden him from entering negotiations with Lalo. The boss hadn't been pleased that he had lied about taking Aston to the containers or that he had agreed to let her take the car's place as collateral.

Writing her another letter to let her know Baby was lost and asking one of the family's runners to deliver it to Aston had been one of the lowest moments of his life. He might have come through on his promise to save her from her stepbrother, but he had lost her father's car. Staring at it now, he wondered what game the boss was playing.

Besian already sat in the passenger seat so Ben slid behind the wheel of the outrageously expensive classic car. He inhaled the crisp scent of the leather and admired the polished wood of the steering wheel with a sweep of his hand. "How?"

"Lalo and I found some common ground, but your blonde honey owned the negotiations. She's tough like her father. I don't think I've ever seen anyone in the cartel fold that easily. Of course, she gave Lalo the choice of any car in her collection."

The pride he had felt at hearing Besian call her tough turned to heartache when he imagined how much it must have hurt her to give away more of her father's things. "Lalo never should have had this one. The drug debt wasn't hers to pay. This car wasn't Calvin's to use as collateral either. She never owed us a debt."

"Her family owed the debt. Calvin is gone. You and Devil made sure of that. I can't collect a debt on an unmarked grave." Besian reached for his seat belt. "I thought you would be proud of her. She pays her debts and has a great deal of integrity and honor. Most women in her position would have simply called the police. She could have used her contacts to bury us."

Fastening his lap belt, Ben wondered why she hadn't done that. Was it because she hadn't wanted him to get hurt? He shoved down the hope that flared to life within him. No, she would have had to answer a lot of uncomfortable questions about Calvin if she had called the police. This wasn't about protecting him. It was about protecting herself and preventing a scandal.

But even as he thought that, he had a hard time believing it.

"Earlier today, she sent me four cars to settle up what she owes with us. Zee will like them. They should be easy to move." Besian gestured that he was ready to go. "That garage her father built is amazing. Did you know she does all the maintenance herself? She's handy with a wrench and quite a mechanic."

"I didn't know that." His fingers tightened around the wheel as he pulled away from the curb. He didn't know, but he *wanted* to know. He wanted to know all of her secrets and quirks. He wanted to be the one she whispered her dreams to in the dark and the one she turned to for help. To hear Besian recounting the small and intimate details about the woman he couldn't forget was like a knife to the heart. Of course, a knife would have been kinder and quicker than the torment he now suffered.

"You look like shit. When was the last time you slept?"

Ben shrugged and kept his gaze fixed on the windshield. "A couple of days."

"Four, I would guess," the boss said knowingly. "Not since you left that girl of yours."

"She's not mine." He hated the sullen tone that invaded his voice.

"So I take it you're not planning to pull a Sergei on me and leave me high and dry over some woman?" The story of the Russian enforcer and prize fighter leaving the mob after his woman bought his debt to the family was still the buzz of Houston's underworld. That Nikolai had given his blessing was even more of a shock.

He cast an incredulous look Besian's way. "How could you ask me that? Haven't I always been loyal to you? Haven't I proven that I'll do anything for the family?"

"I've never doubted you." Besian said as they approached a red light. "Not once. *Never.*"

"But?"

"This family," he gestured between them, "can't be a *real* family to you. We can't give you comfort at night. We can't offer you unconditional love. We can't give you children."

At the mention of children, Ben felt shame. Unable to stop himself, he blurted out, "I wasn't *careful* with her."

Besian's shocked expression didn't match his cool reply. "I see."

"It just ...it happened. I couldn't stop it, and she didn't want to stop it. She looked...happy. She smiled at me, and I could tell that she didn't smile like that for everyone." Rubbing the back of his neck, Ben growled with anger. "I shouldn't have been so irresponsible. Look at me! I know better. I've been *that* kid."

"Have you talked to her? If she's in trouble-"

"It's too soon to know, but if she is, I'll take care of her." He didn't give a shit about the rules. If Aston was pregnant, he wasn't walking away from her and the baby. Devil would probably maim him if he was forced to fight his way out of the family, but he would survive the beating.

"She can take care of herself, Ben. She's rich. She's powerful. She'll be a CEO soon."

She doesn't need you. The boss wasn't going to come right out and say it, but that's what he meant.

"What do you want, Ben?"

"I don't know," he grumbled. "I thought I had it all figured out, but I don't know anymore." He glanced at Besian. "What do you want?"

"I want it all."

"You can't have it all."

Besian laughed as they glided through the intersection. "Let me guess. Zee?"

"He's right. There are rules in this life."

"And where's the rule that says you have to be miserable and unhappy?" Besian shook his head. "This is *my* family now. I make the rules. If you want this girl, take her. But," he added with emphasis, "you'll have to give up the shop. I can't risk having you there. On that score, Zee is right. She is too high-profile. We don't need the extra attention on our operation there."

Ben took a moment to really consider it. He could have Aston, if she still wanted him, but he would lose everything he had worked for and built since Besian had put him in the shop at twenty-one. Six years down the drain-for her.

There wasn't even a choice. "I want her."

"Then go fucking get her!"

But what if she doesn't want me? He didn't have the balls to voice that thought aloud. There was only one way to find out and that was to man-up and ask her.

"There aren't any guarantees in life, Arben." The boss didn't often use his full name, but when he did, it was serious so Ben listened carefully. "You hear that shit all the time, you know? No guarantees. Life is too short. But you don't *know* what that really means until you have a fucking hole in your chest, and you're watching your blood pour out of your body onto the dirt. When you're so weak taking a fucking breath is impossible? When you close your eyes and there's no white light? When all you see is the darkness? You *know.*"

Ben tried to breathe quietly as Besian got whatever the hell this was off his chest.

"I've done things..." His voice trailed off, and he shook his head. "I've hurt people. I've made mistakes, and I've sinned." He rubbed his chest. "I'll pay for all of that someday."

Exhaling roughly, Besian caught and held his gaze. "Don't be me, Arben. Don't wake up at thirty-six and discover how fucking empty your life is. Yes, I have money. I have power. I can snap my fingers and have twelve strippers on their knees if I want them, but that's not what I want."

Ben suspected what the boss really wanted was a certain auburn-haired pawn broker with bright blue eyes and a tangled mess of a family.

"Listen, Ben, if you like this girl, if she makes you happy, if you think she might be something special, claim her. Show her that you can be the man she needs. Be good to her and do right by her."

Signaling the end of the discussion, Besian turned his gaze toward his window. Ben drove the rest of the way in silent contemplation. When they reached the private drive that winded toward Aston's white stone mansion with the slate blue roof, he grew nervous. He touched his cheek and remembered the way she had walloped him in his office. Would she hit him again for running away and not calling her? He deserved it and would gladly accept the sting of a good smack if it meant she would touch him again.

The front door opened as he slowed the car to a stop and Aston walked out of her house with Marley at her side. They were laughing and didn't notice him at first. Aston's smile faded at the sight of her beloved Baby. *At the sight of me.*

Realizing this wasn't going to be easy, he killed the engine and inhaled a steadying breath before stepping out of the car. He didn't know what he was going to say. He didn't have anything to offer Aston.

But he had to try.

My heart leapt for joy at the sight of Baby rolling to a stop. The sight of Ben, however, crushed me. He hadn't called or visited. He had just ...left. After everything we had gone through that night, he had just walked away from me.

"Do you want me to stay?" Marley must have sensed my reluctance to be alone with Ben.

"No, I need to do this. I'll be okay."

She nodded with understanding. "Well, call me if you need to talk. I'll be working late at the shop to-night."

"Alone?" I was scared for her to work alone after she had been kidnapped from the shop.

"I'll be fine." She squeezed my hand. "We have new security." She glanced at Besian. "And other protec-tion."

I hugged her close. "Be careful."

"I will." She stepped back and dug for her keys in her purse. "Let me know if you still want to go see a movie tomorrow night." Her gaze skipped to Ben. "If you change your mind, I'll understand."

"We'll see."

Keys in hand, she headed toward her compact hy-brid. She sized up the situation with Ben and Besian and stopped walking. Gesturing toward the mob boss, she asked, "Do you need a ride?"

He seemed surprised by her offer. I could tell he wanted to say yes. His body language screamed for her, but he shook his head and declined. "I'll call one of my men to come get me."

"I'm headed to Abby's. I pass by a couple of your clubs on the way. It's no trouble to drop you off at one of them if that's where you're headed." She hesitated. "It's really the least I could do."

The mob boss finally nodded. "I appreciate it."

She smiled nervously and gave him a wide berth on her way to the driver's side. Watching the fearsome man slide into the passenger seat of the shiny little hybrid made me smile. What would his associates say when he was dropped off at one of his strip clubs in that thing?

As Besian and Marley pulled away from the house, I turned my attention to Ben. He stood awkwardly near Baby, the keys clenched in his fist, and gazed at me with such longing that I wanted to run to him and throw my arms around his neck.

Refusing to forgive and forget that easily, I remained cold and aloof as I closed the distance between us. I held out my hand and arched an eyebrow. Ben gently placed the keys on my palm. The touch of his skin against mine sent a delicious arc up my arm and into my chest, but I ignored my body's reaction.

Closing my fingers around the keys, I rather haughtily remarked, "Well, I suppose four days late is better than never."

"I'm sorry." He blew out a noisy breath. "I am sorry, Aston."

"For the car or for running away from me and leaving me with nothing but a note?"

"All of it," he said. "I'm a criminal asshole who doesn't deserve you."

My irritation with him lessened. "After the rough start you had in life, the odds of you ending up on the right side of the law weren't high."

"I could have done better. I *should* have done better."

"You can change."

He didn't lie to me. "I am what I am, Aston. Sure, maybe, I can get out of the shadiest shit the family does, but I'm in the family until I die. Besian might allow me to fight my way out of the real mobbed-up side of things, but I'll always be under his thumb. *Always.*"

I understood what he was trying to tell me. Still, I needed to know what, exactly, he had done for his family. "Have you ever killed anyone?"

"No. I've never crossed *that* line. Not even with Calvin," he reminded me. "I haven't ever hit a woman or raped or trafficked. I've hurt people. A lot of people," he added sadly. "I've worked as a bouncer in strip clubs, and I've guarded escorts."

I winced at that revelation. "No more of that, Ben. I mean it."

He swept both hands out in front of him. "Done."

"Look, I'm not naive. I know that your *family* comes with you as a packaged deal, but there are other ways for you to be useful to them without being a thief."

His brow furrowed. "How do you figure that?"

"I don't have it totally worked out yet, but I have some ideas. You'll have to trust me."

"I do trust you."

"Then tell me why you ran."

Ben swallowed nervously. He looked as if he wanted to do anything but talk about his feelings. I stood my ground and waited, forcing him to confront whatever it was that had caused him to flee. Finally, he confessed, "I ran because I was scared."

"Of what? Me?"

"I can't have you, but I want you. You're like way up here." His hand rose above his head. "And I'm down there." He scuffed the dirt with the toe of his boot. "I watched you sleep, and I tried to think about how I could be with you, but I didn't have the answer so I took off before it got awkward."

"I would have preferred awkward to the note."

"I know. I should have stayed. I shouldn't have been so afraid to face you, but you make me feel-"

"What?" I asked, anxious to hear the answer. "What do I make you feel?"

He interlaced our fingers and lifted my hand for a kiss. "Hope, Aston. You make me feel *hope."*

I wasn't silly or romantic enough to think that our future was going to be easy. There were going to be some huge obstacles in our path, but I figured that after surviving that crazy first night together, there wasn't much we couldn't overcome if we tried.

"Aston?" Ben eyed me cautiously, almost as if he feared I would send him away with his tail tucked between his legs.

Squeezing his hand, I stepped closer and placed my hand on his chest. I enjoyed the feel of all that hard heat beneath my palm and breathed in the wonderful scent of him. "I still owe you six days and six nights as collateral."

Grinning, he slid his hand down the curve of my spine to settle on my backside. He gave me a playful swat. "Yes, you do."

"After that, we'll have to renegotiate our contract."

He let loose an exaggerated groan. "I don't know about that. Besian tells me you're tough."

"I think you're man enough to handle a tough woman."

He laughed and dipped his head to kiss me. "Yes, I am."

I made him work for that kiss, tugging back and evading his mouth until he finally resorted to clasping my nape in his huge hand and holding me still. I melted into his sensual kiss and slid my arms around his waist. When we separated a long time later, I glanced at Baby and smiled. Taking his hand, I tugged him toward her. "Come on. Let's go for a ride."

He planted his feet and shot mc a warning look. "Let's try to keep the stunt driving to a minimum tonight."

I rolled my eyes. "Quit whining. Get in."

He smacked my bottom again, hard enough that I yelped. The promising look in his intense gaze sent a swarm of butterflies through my belly. When I slipped behind the wheel, I took a moment to simply enjoy Baby. I ran my hands over her dash and the wheel and tried to memorize the leather scent.

"You really love this car." Ben watched me intently, his expression gentle and understanding.

"Some of my best memories were made in this car. I learned to drive right here on this driveway with Daddy sitting in that seat. I took this car to my first drive-in movie over in Hockley and had my first kiss in it. Marley and I took Baby on our first road trip."

"Where did you go?"

"South Padre Island." I smiled at the memories of that trip. Glancing at Ben, I said, "The last time someone sat in the passenger seat with me was the morning Daddy told me he had pancreatic cancer and that it was too far gone. We sat in here and cried together."

The smile Ben had been mirroring as I told him about the good times deflated as I talked about that awful morning. He reached for my hand and dragged it onto his lap. He held it between both of his big paws. "I'm sorry, Aston. How long ago did he pass?"

"Seven months," I said, still feeling the gaping hole he had left behind in my life. "I miss him so much."

"It gets a little easier," he promised. "Mom has been gone for seven years, and I still choke up when I think about her. I'm not consumed by the grief anymore. It takes time."

"I don't want what Calvin did to ruin everything wonderful that's happened in this car. I don't want to think about his stupid, mean face every time I slide behind the wheel."

"You won't."

"How can you know that?"

Ben leaned over and kissed me, pressing all the passion he held for me into the mating of our mouths. When he pulled back, he swept his fingers down my face. "Because you and I are going to make so many new memories," he swore. "You, me and Baby? We're going places." That sinful, sexy grin of his made my tummy flutter. His hand cupped my knee and moved slowly up my thigh. "I can think of a few memories I'd like to make tonight."

Swallowing hard, I turned the key in the ignition and smiled when Ben fastened my seat belt for me. As I rolled down the driveway, his rough fingers slipped under my skirt and headed for my panties. I let my thighs fall open and inhaled a shaky breath when his fingers dipped under the sheer lace.

Idling at that first stop sign, I turned into his seeking kiss. His fingertips finally found their mark, and I whimpered. Ben nibbled my lower lip before pulling back to gaze at me with such tenderness. "Where are you taking me?"

"I have no idea," I admitted with a laugh.

He kissed my neck. "That's okay. As long as we're together, I'm happy."

Infected by Ben's hope for our future, I smiled at him and eased on the gas. I really didn't have any idea where we would end up, but I suspected we were going to enjoy every second of our journey.

Aston and Ben's story will continue in **COLLATERAL II** coming Fall 2014.

AN AUTHOR'S NOTE

I hope you enjoyed Aston and Ben's tale! Their story will continue with a sequel, COLLATERAL II, releasing Fall 2014.

The *Debt Collection* series focuses on Besian Beciraj'screw. It includes COLLATERAL (available now in ebook and print) and the upcoming books COL**LATERAL** II, **PAST DUE, PAID IN FULL, DOWN PAYMENT** and **FINAL INSTALLMENT.**

This series is a spinoff from my bestselling *Her Russian Protector* books that include **IVAN,DIMITRI, YURI, NIKOLAI, SERGEI, SERGEI** II and **NIKOLAI**

II. Upcoming books in 2014 include new tales for Kostya, Alexei and Danila.

Characters from the *Debt Collection* and *Her Russian Protector* series also make appearances in *The Fighting Connollys,* a trilogy that focuses on brothers Kelly, Jack and Finn, three Marines fighting to save their family legacy and to protect the women they love. **IN KELLY'S CORNER, IN JACK'S ARMS,** and **IN FINN'S HEART** are available now in ebook and print.

ABOUT THE AUTHOR

A *New York Times* and *USA Today* bestselling author, I like to write super sexy romances and scorching hot erotica. I live in Texas with a husband who could easily snag a job as an extra on History Channel's new *Viking* series and a sweet but rowdy preschool-aged daughter.

I also have another dirty-book writing alter ego, Lolita Lopez, who writes deliciously steamy tales for Ellora's Cave, Forever Yours/Grand Central, Mischief/Harper Collins **UK,** Siren Publishing and Cleis Press.

You can find me online at www.roxierivera.com.

Roxie's Backlist

Her Russian Protector

Ivan (Her Russian Protector #1)

Dimitri (Her Russian Protector #2)

Yuri (Her Russian Protector #3)

A Very Russian Christmas (Her Russian Protector #3.5)

Nikolai (Her Russian Protector #4)

Sergei (Her Russian Protector #5)

Sergei, Volume 2

Nikolai, Volume 2 (Her Russian Protector #6) Coming June 2014

Kostya (Her Russian Protector #7)-Coming Summer 2014

Alexei (Her Russian Protector #8)-Coming Fall 2014

Danila (Her Russian Protector #9)-Coming Fall 2014

The Fighting Connollys

In Kelly's Corner (Fighting Connollys #1)

In Jack's Arms (Fighting Connollys #2)

In Finn's Heart (Fighting Connollys #3

Debt Collection

Collateral (Debt Collection #1)

Collateral II (Debt Collection #2)-Coming Soon

Past Due (Debt Collection #3)-Coming Soon

Paid in Full (Debt Collection #4)-Coming Soon

Down Payment (Debt Collection #5)-Coming Soon

Final Installment (Debt Collection #6)-Coming Soon

Her SEAL Protector

Close Quarters

Seduced By...

Seduced by the Loan Shark
Seduced by the Loan Shark 2-Coming Soon!
Seduced by the Congressman
Seduced by the Congressman 2

Erotica

Chance's Bad, Bad Girl
Halftime With Craig
Tease
Eddie's Cuffs 1
Eddie's Cuffs 2
Eddie's Cuffs 3

COLLATERAL

Disturbing the Peace
Quid Pro Quo
Search and Seizure

Made in the USA
Columbia, SC
29 April 2024

35050476R00086